Crime Time
Stories of Crime and Mystery

Dale T. Phillips

Crime Time

Try these other works by Dale T. Phillips

Shadow of the Wendigo (Supernatural Thriller)
Neptune City (Mystery)
Locust Time (Suspense)
Desert Heat (Mystery- coming Spring 2023)

The Zack Taylor Mystery Series
A Darkened Room
A Sharp Medicine
A Certain Slant of Light
A Shadow on the Wall
A Fall From Grace
A Memory of Grief

Story Collections
The Big Book of Genre Stories (Different Genres)
Halls of Horror (Horror)
Deadly Encounters (3 Zack Taylor Mystery/Crime Tales)

1

*The Return of Fear (*Scary Stories*)*
*Five Fingers of Fear (*Scary Stories*)*
*Jumble Sale (*Different Genres*)*
*Crooked Paths (*Mystery/Crime*)*
*More Crooked Paths (*Mystery/Crime*)*
*The Last Crooked Paths (*Mystery/Crime*)*
*Fables and Fantasies (*Fantasy*)*
*More Fables and Fantasies (*Fantasy*)*
*The Last Fables and Fantasies (*Fantasy*)*
*Strange Tales (*Magic Realism, Paranormal*)*
*Apocalypse Tango (*End of the World*)*

Non-fiction Career Help
How to be a Successful Indie Writer
How to Improve Your Interviewing Skills

With Other Authors
Rogue Wave: Best New England Crime Stories 2015
Red Dawn: Best New England Crime Stories 2016
Windward: Best New England Crime Stories 2017

Sign up for my newsletter to get special offers
www.daletphillips.com

DEDICATION

For the great pulp writers of crime and adventure

Crime Time

CONTENTS

Dale T. Phillips

A Little Rest

Francine Merriweather

I've lived a long life. A good one, though now at seventy-eight years old, you'd think I could finally have some time to myself, get a little rest. But my family left me money, and the conditions of the estate trust make many demands, with attorneys, financial advisers, various company bigwigs and board committees all demanding I personally address this or that issue. My assistants try to deal with much of this, but so much gets through to claim what little time I have left that it exhausts me. I sleep very little, unable to relax for any length of time.'

Far worse, though, are the remaining members of the Merriweather clan, all the unpleasant, bickering relations that incessantly clamor and importune me for money. They're a pack of snarling hyenas and jackals, constantly nipping at my heels, looking for a way to bite off a chunk of the estate for themselves. They pray for my demise, so they can feast on the remains. Their attorneys circle like vultures, looking for any sign of weakness, so they can swoop in and declare me incompetent.

And then there's the never-ending flood of charitable organizations badgering me for a bequest to this or that foundation. I've given hundreds of thousands of dollars to various causes, and still they want more, always more. They look on the estate as a giant slot machine that can spill forth a mountain of treasure if they just pitch the correct way.

Some time away was just what I needed. I told no one where I was going. None of the guests at the Greene Mountain Resort are of my circle. Here I can relax, enjoy leisurely meals in solitude, and stroll around the resort gardens and grounds. Finally just sit and read a book. Peace and quiet.

Benny

Man, working as a waiter here is tough. Everything's nice for the rich old guests, but the shabby housing we staff get (for which the resort gets a sweet tax write-off) is a firetrap. For the privilege of our room and board, I get up at seven and work six days a week, three meal shifts every day, until like nine at night. Wears me out. Cheap shoes are all I can afford, and I get shin splints from being on my feet so much.

And hey, at twenty-four, I like to have a little fun, so there's often a bar or a party to go to after our dinner shift is done. But it makes getting up and being cheerful the next morning an exercise in acting, as a couple of days a week I'm usually hung over and seriously sleep-deprived. But since income is all tips from the diners, cheerfulness is the order of the day if you want to make any money.

There's only a short break between the breakfast and lunch shift, and a slightly longer one after lunch, before the big dinner rush. If the guests are done eating, I can clear and reset my section early, and be out of the dining room soon after the meal time is over. Guests who come in late or hang around are always a major pain in the ass, and they're the types that usually demand more and tip less.

I'd been burning the candle at both ends for weeks, and it was catching up with me. It doesn't help that the cook in the room next door to my thin-walled dorm room likes to blast loud death-metal late into the night, making it impossible to sleep anyway. You can't complain, because a number of the staff in the kitchen are all related, and if you get one of them in trouble, you'll never see your meals on time again, or anywhere near the way you requested it. So if you can't sleep, you might as well go out and enjoy yourself, right?

Francine

I arrived at the resort at nine in the evening, and was in bed soon after. Whether it was the mountain air, or my exhaustion, I slept in, for the first time in weeks. In the morning, I went straight downstairs for something to eat. The posted meal times of the dining room says they stop serving breakfast at ten, and I just made it. The hostess took me to my assigned seat of the dining room, where I can look out over the mountain valley and take it all in. It's so beautiful, I could stay here for hours.

Benny

I've been watching for the new guest all morning, and cheered silently when she didn't show up, because it meant I could get out of here for a few minutes before I have to return for the lunch shift. We don't get an hourly wage, only getting paid a dollar a head per meal for each person we wait on, so being on your feet for another hour for one person isn't worth it. You want to pop out as soon as you can, and sit for a few before coming back for the lunch crowd.

I came back from the kitchen, ready to go, and saw the woman being seated in MY section. Mary, the hostess, went straight over from seating her and put up the Closed sign for the dining room. I went over to her.

"Can we put her in someone else's section? Allison's still got guests."

Mary shook her head. "That's your section, Benny, and her assigned seat. She'll be here for a few weeks."

Damn it. I went over to the woman. "Hello, Ma'am, my name is Benjamin, and I'll be taking care of you. Would you like some coffee?"

"Tea," she replied.

"Coming right up. Here's our breakfast menu."

"I didn't want to order just yet."

I looked toward the doors leading out from the dining hall. The staff out there hate late orders and blame us waiters when we put one in.

"Yes, Ma'am, it's just that the kitchen puts the breakfast things away right about now."

"I was told if I was seated, I could get my meal as I liked. Is that not the case?"

I was thinking vile thoughts, but I smiled. "I'll make sure you get what you need."

Coffee we can pour from the pots on burners out in the dining room, but I went out to the kitchen to get the tea, muttering curses under my breath the whole time. Rich-bitch pain in the ass. I stuck a bag into a metal tea pot, filled it with hot water from the urn, and brought it back out and set it down. The menu was still on the other side of the table, where I'd left it.

She looked up. "There's no lemon. I'd like some lemon with it, please. And some honey."

I almost swore out loud. Why hadn't she asked for the lemon and the honey when she ordered the tea? Now I had to go all the way back out to the kitchen. I made the long trek back and went to the walk-in cooler for the lemon. Damn her. I looked at the yellow wedge and rubbed it in my armpit before putting it on a small plate. That'll teach her. I found an empty creamer jug and spit in it, then got the honey and poured out a portion into the jug. I returned to the dining room and set the plate with the lemon down before her, and the honey jug. "Are you ready to order, Ma'am?"

She sniffed. "This tea is not hot. I would like it hot, please."

I forced a smile and picked up the cup and the pot.

Back to the kitchen, where George was behind the metal counter (the "line") on the broiler station, and he was okay.

"Hey George, lady says her tea's not hot. Mind heating these up for her?"

George smiled and took the cup, saucer, and pot and slid them on a rack inside the broiler. I went to get a small round tray and a kitchen towel. I came back soon after and passed the tray over the counter. George slid a spatula under each piece and removed them, setting them on the tray.

"See how she likes that." George cackled, showing a couple of missing teeth.

I gave him a thumbs up and went back out. I used the towel to set down each item. "That cup is very hot, Ma'am, so you be careful now."

"Certainly took you long enough." She looked around. "It's not like you're busy."

"No, Ma'am, as you can see, we're the only ones left here now."

She gave me a sharp look. Well, there goes the probably-forty cent tip she was going to leave me. "Are you being impertinent?"

"Whatever do you mean, Ma'am?" I had my bland face on, with my most soothing voice. If she complained, it wasn't good. Here, the customer is always right, no matter how big an asshole they are.

She took the handle of the pot. "Ow."

"Is something wrong?"

"This pot is red hot."

"Sorry, Ma'am. It's the only way to make sure the tea is as hot as you requested."

She pursed her lips and drew a long sigh. "I see. That's how it is. Then I'd like to order now."

Hallelujah, I thought.

"I'd like half a grapefruit, scrambled eggs, very dry, and whole wheat toast, unbuttered. And a small glass of prune juice."

"Yes Ma'am, coming right up." I started to leave, but she spoke again.

"Make sure those eggs are very dry."

'As dry as you, you dried-up old bitch,' I thought.

I returned to the kitchen and went to the egg station. Fat Chris was in that spot today, and he's a dick to work with. He hates everybody, but waiters in particular.

"One order scrambled, very dry." I put an empty plate up on the rack to verify the order.

"Breakfast is over," Chris said, glowering at me.

"Wish it was so. Blame Mary, who seated her, and said we have to serve her."

The sweating Chris muttered under his breath, as if I was the one to blame for ruining his day.

I went to another cooler for the prune juice and the grapefruit, both of which would have been more accessible during the breakfast rush. I put a gob of spit on the grapefruit and spread it around with my finger. Back out to the dining room to plonk down the grapefruit and the juice.

No conversation this time. Maybe she'd learned her lesson after getting burned.

Back out to the kitchen, where I had to go to the cooler again to find another loaf of whole wheat bread. I took out two slices and wiped them on the counter before putting them in the toaster. Then I went back to the egg station. "Picking up."

Chris shoved a plate onto the rack and watched me. The eggs were loose and runny, despite that I'd ordered them dry. Remembering the white-clad mafia mindset of

the kitchen crew, I decided not to fight it. Instead, I went
back to George.

"George, we need to dry these puppies out some. Can
we use your broiler again?"

He laughed. "Got a real ball-buster, huh?"

I made a face. "You wouldn't believe."

Back over to the toaster. When the toast popped out,
I plated it and topped it with a tin cover. It wouldn't
help much to keep it warm, but she would at least be
able to see I was doing all I could. Then over to pick up
the eggs, cover them with a plastic topper, and back out
to the big empty dining room.

"Here you go, Ma'am. Careful, that plate is hot."

"I'm sure it is," she said. "But as you can see, I'm
not done with my grapefruit yet."

I had a mental flash of me shoving the grapefruit into
her face, like James Cagney did to Mae Clarke in that
old movie The Public Enemy. But she wasn't worth
getting fired over.

"No problem, Ma'am, I'll take that away. Just let
me know when you're ready."

I took the eggs and the toast back out to the kitchen.
Why in hell had this old bitch been seated in my section?
My feet hurt, and I needed to sit, so I went out to the
back loading dock and sat on the concrete. I had a
smoke. After a few minutes, I got up and went back out
to the kitchen. I had George slide the plate of eggs under
the broiler, and dropped in two more slices of toast before

13

going back to the dining room, to make sure she was finally fucking done with her goddamn grapefruit.

"Where have you been?" The old bitch looked to be quivering with anger. "I've been wanting my breakfast."

"Coming right up," I said, and wheeled back around to the kitchen. When George gave me the plate, I took them off to the side. I stirred the eggs up with a fork so they wouldn't look as if they had baked, and covered them. I grabbed the toast, covered it, and brought at all back out and set it down on the table, and removed the covers

The woman peered at the plate. "Are these the same eggs?"

"No Ma'am, I had them cook you up a fresh batch." Yeah, like they'd do that.

"They don't look fresh."

"They don't, when they're scrambled very dry like that."

She sighed. "I am upset now, and find my appetite is gone. Please take them away."

I knew she was playing games with me. "Will there be anything else, Ma'am?"

"I don't think I have time to wait that long, I'm afraid," she gave me a poisonous smile.

And just like that, the war was on.

Francine

I did not run a multi-million dollar foundation by being a pushover. When I wanted things done, I got them done, by whatever means. When people opposed me, well, I had years of experience in removing obstacles. And I made people pay for getting in my way. This rude young man had ruined my first morning, and kept me from relaxing. So I went to the hostess and told her how polite and efficient he was, and I hoped I would have him as a server for every meal.

For the next three days, I came in for every meal just before the hostess closed the dining room, and sat long after the other guests had gone. My reward was seeing the young man seethe with hatred and anger when he served me, knowing I had enormous power over him. I made him go for extra trips, take food back that wasn't cooked to my specifications, and made a complete nuisance of myself.

But it cost me as well. My constitution at this age was a touch on the delicate side, and all the stomach acid I built up in these little battles made my digestion suffer. But as I did not allow myself to view my actions as harmful to myself in any way, I naturally thought it was something done to me by my server.

I accosted him after I had been forced to miss a meal due to stomach distress. "Young man, are you poisoning my food?"

"What?" He looked at me with mouth open.

"My food. You're putting poison in it. You want to kill me."

The young man shook his head, turned, and walked away.

Benny

For days she's been playing her old bitch game, making me hang around the dining room just for her. Nothing is good enough, either, as she makes me run and run for extras, for returned food, for any excuse whatsoever. I was so tired, and she just wore me down. Someone else told me an old trick of putting a few drops of an over-the-counter medication into her food to make her just a little sick, maybe enough so she wouldn't come in for a meal or two, but I hadn't done it.

And one glorious meal, she hadn't come in. I rejoiced, and was out of the dining room soon after the meal ended. It was wonderful having a few minutes off, and it pissed me off to think of how much of my time she's wasted, that rich old bat. She could do anything, could go anywhere, and she chooses to fritter away chunks of the remaining part of her life sitting in a big dining room so some schmuck of a waiter has to waste his own time.

But the next meal she was back, and she was glaring at me worse than usual. When I went over, she accused me of poisoning her. I walked away, muttering curses. Why did this crazy broad have to get stuck in my section? She should be committed.

Francine

Being ill made me realize that I might not have much time left. At seventy-eight, it could be any moment. I smiled to think of leaving life while engaged in my lone little battle, even if my opponent wasn't much to brag about.

Very well, if he was going to do me in, I would let him- but I would have her revenge. I made many calls, and got important men to come to the resort and sit with me to go over stacks of paperwork. Ignoring my desire to rest, instead I busied herself with numerous affairs of the trust. My lawyers drew up contracts and had me sign them, while they exchanged glances on the sly.

Working continuously further affected my health. I could barely eat anymore, but I willed herself to go to the dining room and sit, grimly issuing orders for many dishes that I didn't touch. The young man seemed barely able to restrain himself.

17

I finally broke down and was confined to my room on doctor's orders, and then he demanded I seek hospital treatment. I tried to resist, but the terms of the trust forced me to have to follow a certain cause of action in special circumstances. I left the resort, sparing one backward glance at my last vacation site.

Benny

When the woman didn't come in for a meal, I was happy. When she was absent for the following one, I was ecstatic. I went out that night to celebrate, and was so hung over the next morning I could barely see. I was expecting to encounter her grim visage, but was told she had left the resort on doctor's orders. I felt a little guilty about what I had finally put in her food, but it was after she'd accused me of poisoning her. Very well, if she wanted to be made sick, I'd finally obliged.

It was several weeks later that the lawyers came back to the resort with grave faces and full briefcases. They met with me in one of the big meeting rooms, to inform me that as a beneficiary of the estate of Francine Merriweather, I was now a wealthy man, provided I take over the business of the trust and abide by the rules set down. They explained things, but my head reeled from the enormity of what had happened. The old woman had indeed been crazy, and left me a chunk of money to continue her work. Giggling and giddy, I signed each sheaf of paperwork they put before me. I had no idea it was a trap.

I quit the resort, and for a week, I celebrated in style, but eventually more lawyers came by and read me the riot act. They showed me my signature on a contract that stipulated rules of conduct. I was to now be monitored by a panel of board members, who would see that I behaved, and spend the requisite number of hours dealing with trust business, and attend all pertinent meetings.

And the lawsuits came flooding in. Members of the Merriweather clan were outraged that a stranger had benefited in any way from her estate. They thought every penny of it was rightfully theirs, though I was told the old lady had hated them and fought them off for years. They determined to crush this upstart with a flood of injunctions, and I had to sit for hours every day listening to a team of attorneys explain the latest court proceeding. I was forced to appear in person in court, and endure tedious hours of testimony and bickering over the fact of my elevation to trust office.

She had also given my name to every charitable organization on the planet, it seemed. Forced by the trust agreement to attend public functions, I was buttonholed for money by most people I met, and the constant barrage of requests made me bitter, as if the world saw me as nothing but a human cash machine.

Every day brought more work and more attacks. It was all too much, and I continued to drink heavily. I blew up and told the lawyers I was quitting, giving up the trust oversight and the money, but I had signed agreements. If I left, I would have no more legal counsel, and the estate would join the line of those suing me for breach of contract and malfeasance. As I couldn't disappear, I realized the perfection of the trap she had set. I was rich and supposedly powerful, but her ghost was even more so, and the conditions she'd set down and I had so blithely agreed to now bound me like a steel spiderweb. All I could see was an endless procession of days of torment and tedium, as my strings were pulled like a puppet. She had set the tune, and I must dance to it until the end of my days. Her revenge was complete.

I spent each night exhausted from the battles of the day, seeking only a means of escape, wishing only for a little rest.

***

Chinese Rock

Two in the morning, eyes wide open, I can't sleep. The itch is crawling up my arms, driving me nuts. The craving comes in waves, a throbbing sensation that lets me know how empty I am, how deep my need is. I've tried so hard to hold out, but I know I'm not going to make it. Tonight is not the night I get clean.

Cindy knows. She was crying in the shower stall earlier. She got off the rock when they had her in that place. She's been back a week, and so far hasn't slipped. But she's a lot stronger than me. I can't get off the rock, not for her sake, not for mine. I know I should, it's killing me. Lost my spot in two different bands, and now no one who knows will even let me try out for any openings. But Hell, the music world is packed with rockers: in the old days it was

Coltrane, Chet Baker, Art Pepper, geniuses like that. Now at least one in most bands are using. Sign of the times. Some can control it, some get off it. I can't seem to shake it.

I'm going to have to go out to score, but there's no money and nothing left to pawn or sell. I owe Fang for two already, so he won't front me again. This roach-infested rathole of an apartment has plaster crumbling onto us. There's no appliances, no copper pipes to tear out and sell, no fat marks around to roll. Cindy won't hook for me to get some money, not after all the work she did to get clean. I'm pretty much up against it.

If I had a gun, I could stick up someone or some all-night joint, but the Saturday Night special I'd stolen got pawned last week. I could pretend to have a gun in my pocket, but I'd probably get shot. People are edgy these days, ya know. And at two in the morning, it was going to be damn near impossible to get close enough to strangers on the street. And what idiot is gonna be out with a roll of cash at this time of night? Even the drunks were careful.

Back before Dee-Dee got pinched, he had a lead on a score that we were gonna try. Guy he knew had a garage tucked away out of sight, with a Classic Olds Cutlass in good shape. We were gonna steal it and sell it to Fat Tony at his all-night chop shop. Couldn't steal any newer car nowadays, they got all the fancy ignitions, so you can't just hotwire it or pop one with a screwdriver, like in the old days. And some got kill switches, or even LoJack, or some crap like that. Fat Tony would kill anyone who drove to his place in a hot car and brought the cops right behind.

So yeah, it was the Olds. I'd get a C-note, for sure. Maybe two. Even had a rusty crowbar and a couple of tools stashed. Trouble was, it really was a two-man job. If the owner came out, he had to be distracted long enough for us to get away. Might even have a dog. Guy with a ride like that would wanna protect it, so it was risky, especially by myself. But I was out of options.

Dee-Dee had shown me the place a couple of weeks ago. He'd seen the garage door, with only a big-ass padlock, no alarm. Then he got caught for something else, was now at Riker's. With no money, there was no way was he gonna make bail, so he was there until trial. He'd understand if I took down the score without him. Who knew when he'd get out, after all?

Didn't say anything to Cindy when I left. She was probably awake, but knew there was nothing she could utter that would stop me. She'd been there, even if she was clean for now.

I got the tools from where we'd stashed them. They weren't much, just a broken screwdriver and an old crowbar, but if felt good to have them, almost like I knew what I was doing. I made my way through the streets, still looking for any easier opportunities. There was a group down the block that was real bad news, so I moved carefully, out of sight.

Sometime later, I was near the spot. I went through the trash on the sidewalk, pulling out some old, dried-out newspapers. I found the address, and looked around. Okay, nobody out, that was good. Time to set up my distraction. There was a car parked nearby, all alarmed, of course. But they don't alarm the bottom, and by being real careful, I spiked the gas tank without setting it off. Good thing I didn't have the shakes yet. I used some of the dribbling gas to soak the newspaper, and laid it all flat near the front of the car, gas trailing back towards the tank drip. I took out the stub of candle from my works, and the matches. Saying a prayer, I lit the candle stub and carefully placed it on the newspaper. Figured I'd have maybe five minutes or so before the poof.

Sneaking around back to the garage, I was happy to hear no barking. I got to the door and inspected the padlock. It was a big one. Even if I'd had bolt cutters, I don't think I'd have had the strength to chop that sucker, so it was good I didn't have to. Where the hasp attached to the door, that was the weaker part, and I stuck the pry end of the crowbar in and levered with all my strength. The shriek it made was enough to wake anybody, but it took another minute and more pushing until the screws gave and the whole thing popped loose. I snatched the handle and pulled the door up, sure the owner had heard and was on the way.

A whoosh and a flare of light from the street told me my diversion was now going, and I hoped it would be enough. The Olds was there, sure enough, my ticket to Happyland. I popped the door lock out with the screwdriver, and got behind the wheel. I got the screwdriver into the ignition, but before I could go further, I heard the click of a pistol behind my ear, and I was pinned by a flashlight beam. I froze.

"Don't move, asshole," came a cold voice. "I don't want to clean your brains out of there."

My voice came out in a squeak. "There's a car on fire out there."

"So what?" The man chuckled. "Not my car. You got everyone else's attention, but I'm here to protect what's mine. Now put down that screwdriver and get out real slow. And put your hands up, just like in the movies."

I did like he said, though I wanted to grab the crowbar and take my chances. "Listen, man, no harm done. Just let me go, and you'll never hear from me again. And you won't have to deal with the cops."

He laughed. "My brother-in-law is on the job, so you're screwed, little man. They're already on the way. Although I'd really like to pop you, no lie. I could do it, too, say you jumped me."

At this point, I almost wanted him to do it. I knew what was in store for me. I had priors from a couple of beefs with the law, so there was no chance I'd skate on this one, even volunteering for rehab.

I played my last card. "What if I gave you three grand?" Of course I didn't have it, but if he bought it...

"If you had three grand, you wouldn't be boosting my car now, would you?"

"I know where I can get it. I'll come right back with it, I swear."

"Shut up. How'd you find me here, anyway?"

I kept my trap shut. I was no rat. Dee-Dee had been stealing packages from doorsteps in the neighborhood, and he'd found this place by sheer accident, and seen the Olds inside.

"Look, man, I can't go inside." Even I hated the whine in my voice.

"Sure you can," he said. "Only reason I don't punch your ticket now is because you'll have it a lot worse there."

***

A couple of hours later, the sick was coming on in waves. I'd been slapped around, hauled in, booked, stripped, checked, and was now in a holding cell, with two drunks and a mean-looking bastard who was eyeballing me like I was his next meal. I doubted I'd make it to arraignment.

A uniform came up to the bars and looked us over. He pointed a finger at me. "You. Come with me."

I was shaky, but I could still walk. We stopped at a small room off the corridor, and the cop led me inside. A man was sitting there at a small square table, with a file folder in front of him. The cop pushed me down in a chair across from the man and started to chain me to the ring on the table, but the man waved his hand.

"That won't be necessary, officer. Thank you."

The uniform furrowed his brows, but he left without arguing. So this guy had some juice, for sure.

I blinked. "You my lawyer?" He was dressed like one, and he had a briefcase. "Public defender?"

He smiled. "More like a genie. And you get three wishes. I already know what they are."

I stared at him.

He held up a thumb. "One, get out of this mess somehow." He held up his index finger, ticking the wishes off. "Two, get your next fix. From the looks of it, you're not far from having a pretty bad time." He held up another finger. "And three, get off the junk for good, so you won't end up back here or dead. How did I do?"

I gulped. "Can you help me?"

"I can, if you're ready for it." He tapped the folder. "I've seen your jacket. You've been a bad boy before, but this is the Big Time. Grand Theft Auto and arson. That'll add up to seven years, and that's if the judge is feeling lenient.

Could be ten to fifteen. Think you can do that time? Your life is over."

"So what are you offering?"

"You work for us."

"Who's us?"

"Doesn't matter. We plant a small chip in your head to help with those cravings, so you'll be feeling good, but it won't be the junk. Much healthier. Then we send you out on errands, with a small pen camera to keep track of things."

"What kind of errands?"

"Does it really matter? You stole everything, even purses from little old ladies. You most likely had a hand in that shooting at the convenience store. The guy didn't make it, by the way. Had three kids, too. You don't really care who you hurt, as long as you get your fix. So you come to work for us instead, and you do whatever the hell we tell you to."

I hung my head. No one wants to hear the real truth about themselves. "Why me?"

"Just for being what you are. Completely expendable. You're a junkie loser with nothing more to lose."

"Cindy," I croaked.

"Yeah, that's all over. With you out of the picture, maybe she's got a chance. Being with you was killing her. So if you really care, you'll see this is the best way."

"I'm feeling sick."

"Of course you are," he smiled. He set a small bottle on the table. "This will see you through. Or you could tell me to screw myself and go cold turkey in the cells. Your choice." He set a paper and pen in front of me. "Just sign the agreement."

"Sure you don't want it in blood?"

"A sense of humor. That's good. No, I'm not the devil."

I wasn't sure about that, but I signed anyway.

***

Whatever was in that bottle, it did the trick. My shakes stopped, and though it wasn't as good as Chinese Rock, it was a good ride anyway, making me all fuzzy-headed. Probably the point. Through the guy's magic powers, they released me, and I was taken to a building somewhere. They shaved my head, gave me some more joy juice, and I awoke feeling better and stronger than I had in years. When I reached up to touch the bandages on my head, a stern nurse told me not to. I shrugged and drifted back into oblivion. Which was sure a lot better than Riker's would have been. Anything was better. Or so I thought.

***

They gave me some training I don't remember, and over the next three years, I did a lot of jobs. Most I don't recall, because after every one, they brought me back, and jolted that chip in my head to make me forget. Most of the time I wanted to, because there were faint echoes of nasty things, blood, and screams, and things that are better forgotten. Wisps of memory lingered, just enough to make me loathe myself and what I was doing. I knew I wasn't on the side of the angels. The pen camera let them know every move I made, but I sure as hell didn't want to know what they'd seen. But I had money in my pocket, clean clothes, and a place to live that wasn't a rathole.

The chip controlled me, and kept me off the junk. A current buzzed through my brain, and all was good, all other darkness in the past, a blur of disjointed neurons. Yeah, I was even reading now, and healthy, eating right and getting exercise. They had me dress for some jobs, like a working stiff. No one who'd known me would recognize me now.

At least I thought so.

"Cindy?" The woman was indeed she, looking like a real person, not the wreck she'd been when she was with me. She almost glowed with health.

"Is it really you?" She hugged me. "I didn't recognize you at all."

"Let me look at you," I said. "You did it. You kicked it."

"Looks like you did, too." Her eyes clouded. "I thought you were in jail, or even dead."

"I knew your being with me would drag you down. So I had to leave. You understand that, right?"

She bit her lip and then nodded. "Yeah. But it still hurt."

"I missed you too."

"Was it a program?"

"Of sorts," I shrugged. "Got clean for my new job with a research company. How about you?"

"Yeah, I'm working, too. Cleaning houses for rich people."

"How about that?"

"Hey, listen. I'm on my way to work now, but how about we have lunch tomorrow, really catch up? Here's my number. Just ask for me."

She gave me a card advertising a cleaning service.

"We'll do that."

I was humming to myself afterward, glad that she had made it, had a real life now. It made everything all right, even the crap I was doing now all worth it. Hell, maybe we could even get back together. Anything was possible.

My employers called very early the next morning and told me to come in. When I got there, the man who gave me the forgetting shocks and new instruction was there. He pointed to a chair. "Sit down." I did. "What did you think you were doing?"

"What do you mean?"

"Engaging that woman in conversation."

"Cindy? I knew her before."

"Exactly. Now she's a liability."

"How? I didn't tell her anything."

The man's face was red. "We operate on absolute secrecy. You could expose us."

"It's no big deal."

"Oh, but it is." The man put an automatic and a suppressor on the table. "So you're going to have to take care of it."

I looked at the gun, and then back up at him. "You're kidding."

"We are dead serious. You have to end the relationship. Permanently."

I shook my head. "No. You can't. Not just because we met by chance."

"You can, and you will."

He left the room, and a few minutes later, my senses bloomed with white light. The man came back and spoke to me. I put the gun and suppressor in my pocket and went out.

I found where Cindy worked. She came in at nine, looking great. I had the gun wrapped in a plastic trash bag, and was wearing a wig. I came up behind her and put two shots into the back of her head. She fell without a sound. I walked away, and ditched the gun in pieces in storm drains two blocks away.

With the assignment done, I had a bit of myself back temporarily, and I broke down sobbing, horrified at what I'd done. They'd wipe it out later, but for the moment I was lost, melting away as I realized what they'd done to me, to make me kill the only person I ever cared about. I didn't want this anymore, didn't want to live with them controlling me as a puppet. I threw the pen camera to the ground and smashed it with my foot.

In my former life, I knew where to go to score. I found a guy without any problem, and soon had some prime snortable powder in hand. The chip was still pushing me to return the base, but when I took the powder, the old rush overwhelmed the programming. It hit me hard, and I realized how much I'd missed it. I was flying. I made my way down to the subway, while the chip in my head buzzed like wasps.

I'd show them. Standing at the edge of the platform, I felt the onrushing train, and knew it was my release. From the rock, from the company, and from everything I'd done. I was free again.

I stepped forward.

***

Dale T. Phillips

Family Affair

Marla bit her nails as she watched the news. She kept flicking her gaze to the suitcases of money. She and her husband Jeb had transferred the cash from the bank bags, which he was now burning in a barrel out back, along with the clothes and masks they'd worn. Since the money came from an armored car pickup, there had been no dye packs, transponders, or fake bills to worry about. They'd already ditched the guns off a bridge into deep water. All but one.

Denise sat on the couch, her tears mostly dried by now. "Mom, quit pacing. How many times can I say I'm sorry?"

Marla shook her head, her mouth in a tight line. "It was supposed to be *perfect*, Denny. Just you, me, and your dad. A family affair. Why'd you have to tell *him?*"

"Rafe knew we were planning, mom. He said when you've been inside, you get a sense for what's going on, like when someone's planning a heist. He kept after me, said he'd lock me up unless I told him. He was watching me so close, I couldn't have broke away to help you. It would have screwed us up."

"He *did* screw us up, Denny. Jesus. Some money ripped off, that's insured. They look, but not so hard as now. When someone's shot, they take it personal. They'll never stop looking. We'll have to leave, say goodbye to this house, and hide out for years. I liked this place. It was safe. You, your dad and I have one cardinal rule on a job. *No killing.* He agreed, and then went ahead and did it anyway."

"I know, it went all wrong. We still got away, though."

Marla threw up her hands. "Yeah. *For now.* He damned sure got enough people looking at us after he shot those men. What if someone saw his tattoos, or something else to identify him? How long will it take the cops to hone in on an ex-con stickup man in town? And you know he'll roll on us in a second, anything to get himself a lighter sentence. Son of a bitch would even claim one of *us* did the shooting."

"So what do we do now?"

"We give him his share and say goodbye, while we go find a safe place where the cops won't find us."

Rafe came into the room, a bottle of beer in hand like he was any regular guy at home on a Saturday afternoon. "Talking about me?"

Marla shot him a poisonous look.

Rafe took a swig of beer and belched. "Heard you both. How you're gonna ditch me. You and the old man can split, but Denny's coming with me. We make a good team."

Marla shot a glance at Denny, who looked scared. "And you want *her* share as well as yours. You're careless, you're going to get caught. Look at you, still walking around with the gun you used to kill those men. They catch you with that, you ride the needle. I don't want Denny going down with you."

Rafe tapped the revolver tucked in the front of his pants. "I like this gun. And don't worry, we ain't gonna get caught."

"Says the man who did a nickel in Raiford."

"Don't get smart with me. I know what I'm doing."

"That why you shot the guards?"

He shrugged. "Guy wasn't moving fast enough."

"And his partner?"

"Collateral damage." Rafe dropped into the easy chair. "Babe, get me another beer, willya?"

Marla cursed. "You're some piece of work."

"You never liked me. Think you're better. But you're all criminals, just like me."

"We're *nothing* like you. You're a murderer."

"Whatever. You might want to start counting out half of that money. Denny and I are leaving tonight."

"With the cops all out looking. You're dumber than I thought."

"Watch your mouth, old woman. Or I just might take *all* the money."

Behind Rafe, Denny cooed. "You know I love you babe, right?"

"Sure."

"But *family* is more important." She swung the baseball bat across the back of his skull with a hard thunk.

Marla smiled proudly at her daughter.

***

Gumshoe

In Room 101, the windowless interrogation parlor of the police station, the paint peeled in lead snowflakes from the walls, while an unseemly reek offended the air. The odor might have been from years of sweat, desperation, and flatulence, or perhaps it was the wafting breeze from the nearby break-room microwave, where some idiot had heated their early lunch of leftover fish.

A heavily-bandaged man slumped in the hard chair while securely handcuffed to the metal ring on the table. Fresh scars and bruises decorated his weather-beaten face, and he looked like someone who had fallen down a long flight of stairs, and in the process, lost a winning lottery ticket.

Detective Rochambeau adjusted the notepad and pen before him and spoke into a digital recorder. "This is the statement of one Marlow Spenser, private investigator, arrested for the murder of Wensleydale Colby. Today is the 12th of June, the time is eleven-oh-three, and present are Detective Lafayette Rochambeau, that's me, and Detective Niles List."

Rochambeau sat back and eyed the man across the table. "Go ahead with your statement."

The bandaged man shook his head. "I didn't do it. It was all *his* fault. Everything. That moron ruined my life. And now this." He shook the cuffed wrist, which rattled against the ring.

"I guess I better start at the beginning." He eyed the recorder. "You'd better get some fresh batteries for that thing, because this is going to take a while." He looked around. "Can I get a cup of coffee, or a soda?"

Detective List left the room and soon returned with a paper cup.

Spenser took a sip and winced. "This tastes like motor oil mixed with battery acid."

List shrugged. "We drink it all the time here."

"Not surprising. How hard is it to make decent coffee? Is it impossible to get anyone who's barely competent? I'm beginning to think so, after all that's happened."

Rochambeau cleared his throat. "Why don't we get back to your statement? The sooner we finish, the sooner you can get back to your cell."

"Oh, yay. The crowded room where half of them want to pound on me because the guard said my *badge* looked fake. He didn't tell them I'm a *Private Investigator*, not a cop, but now they all think I'm a police plant. So sure, let's rush on to my next beating."

Spenser took another sip from the cup, made a face, and put it aside. He sighed like a farmer surveying a field of ruined crops.

"It all began when I was hired by Mrs. Dunning-Kruger…"

Rochambeau looked up from where he'd already been doodling on the notepad. "The governor's wife?"

"Yeah. She hired me to help her son, Ignatius Junior."

"With a name like that, he sounds like he needed help."

"You don't know the half of it. He tells people to call him '*AJ*', because he thinks his first name starts with an '*A*'. He's an incompetent idiot, a total tool. Always has been, but the mother has worked to keep that knowledge from him. So he's cocky as hell, got an inflated opinion of what he can do, and thinks he's an expert in just about everything. He's got a display case full of sports trophies and medals from rigged tournaments his mother set up, including the one where he "won" his Black Belt in Karate. He has a diploma from an Ivy League school, courtesy of a fat check from the Dunning-Kruger Foundation. His girlfriends, all supermodels or actresses, were hired after being carefully screened by mother, but he thinks he's a real Don Juan, despite that stupid haircut, the big nose, and the lazy eye. Even his car, for the love of Mike."

Rochambeau frowned. "Who's Mike?"

Spenser rolled his eyes. "It's just an expression."

"Oh. Go on. What about the car?"

"His mother spent half a mil on it. It's self-driving, with extra safety features built in to avoid *any* type of collision. Kid's never had an accident, so he thinks he's an expert driver. He's *caused* plenty, but never got his own vehicle hit.

"And *everybody* flatters him, because they want to suck up to the favored son of the Governor. His ego is monstrous. He goes out for dinner to a restaurant, he always sends the wine back, know what I mean?

"Anyway, Mrs. Dunning Kruger summoned me to a meeting, on the QT."

Rochambeau stopped doodling. "What's the QT? A ship?"

Spenser sighed loudly. "It's another expression, a shortened form of 'quiet.' It means to meet in secret. She didn't want anyone to know."

Rochambeau nodded and went back to his doodle, a drawing of the car Kitt, from the television show *Knight Rider*.

Spenser looked at the coffee cup, shook his head, and went on.

"So the kid watches *The Maltese Falcon* on TV one night, falls in love with it, and tells Mommie Dearest he wants to be a Private Eye, just like Sam Spade. She knows he can't even solve the case of how his shoes came untied, so she asks around and gets my name as someone good at their job. I meet her, and she wants me to metaphorically hold Junior's hand while I teach him how to be a Private Eye. And of course, he'll get to solve some cases that have

45

me stumped. All part of the game. At first, I said no, but she warned me that her husband could get my PI license suspended, and she took out an envelope with a hundred G's in cash. Said there's be more when the kid was happy and moved on to something else. Well, I've never seen that much money at once, so I swallowed my pride and took the cash. What a fool I was."

"Why's that?"

"It started my ride to Hell. I set up a supposed chance meeting with the kid and had him solve the case of the missing phone. Although I almost had to pound the answer into his forehead, I pretended to be amazed at his deductive powers, and said he'd make a crackerjack PI, and would he consider being my partner. Any fool would have seen that it was a setup, but he fell for it, hook, line, and sinker. We went to the gun range, and he shot a perfect score- except he was firing blanks, and the holes in the target were pre-drilled. Mommy greased some wheels at the state level and he was issued a PI license, something that really torqued me off. I had to work hard for mine, and here this clown gets one by *buying* it. He was a real gumshoe, all right. If there was gum anywhere on the ground, or dog crap, for that matter, he'd step in it.

"So then Mommy paid for a comfy office that we could work out of. He went out and bought what he thought was a statue of a Maltese Falcon, but it's actually a stuffed owl. Hard as hell keeping a straight face when he brought that back and set it up.

"We had an actress playing our secretary, Velma, and the script was that she would quickly fall for him. We kept bottles of booze in our desks, so watered down it was like lemonade, and part of the act was that we'd be hard-drinking tough guys who poured bourbon in our morning coffee. He thought he could handle his liquor. Truth was, two stiff drinks and he'd pass out."

Spenser twisted his mouth up while he gave a sour look at the paper cup. "Maybe if you added some real bourbon to that mess, it might taste better."

List spoke up. "Who says we don't?"

Rochambeau gave a shocked glance at his partner before settling his gaze on Spenser. "Then what happened?"

"Well, we had to create some cases for him to solve. Not an easy task, because he was a dimwit. We'd have to plant obvious clues, and

I'd have to lead him to the answer like he was on a leash, and then rub his nose in it. I say all that, because his first case was a missing dog. I had my girlfriend's Labrador, and she came in posing as a new client and asked if he could find her dog for her. Slam dunk, because I had the mutt in a crate, ready to spring it, and let the dope recover it.

"The dog had a collar and name tag, and she gave him a picture for a perfect ID. I let the mutt go in the hallway of our floor, and asked Iggy if he heard any barking. He checked it out, said there was a dog in the hallway, and came back in and sat down. Grinding my teeth, I asked if it could it be the dog she was looking for? He said he didn't think so. I said to check the dog's collar to be sure, so he did it, pouting the whole time, and finally came back with the dog."

Spenser blew his breath out. "So I call our 'client' to tell her to come down, that Iggy had found her dog. We celebrate our first case success with some watered bourbon. I hit the can, and when I come back, I don't see the mutt. When I ask where it is, he points out the open window. He was playing with the thing, threw a small rubber ball, but it bounced out the window, and the dumb dog went after it.

Luckily, our office was on the first floor. Last he saw of the dog, it was running hell-for-leather down Mulberry Street. Animal Control nabbed it an hour later, and my girlfriend had to go pay a fine to get him back, and listen to a lecture about responsible dog ownership. She *still* won't talk to me."

Spenser shifted in the chair. "So lesson learned, no more cases involving live animals. Then I thought, 'how about a bike'? I arranged for a guy playing a messenger to come ask us to get his delivery bicycle back. Again, we had a picture, so there couldn't be any mistake. What does this jerk do? We go to the park, where I've stashed the bike, but he sees a little girl riding *her* bike, wasn't even the same *color*, and accuses her of stealing. Her father's there, and when she starts crying, he beats the crap out of me, despite the fact I'm the one trying to explain how it's all a mistake. Busted two of my ribs, I had to go to the hospital. By the time I get back to the park, somebody's found the bike I stashed and took it."

Spenser paused. "Hey, I've been talking a while. How about some lunch?"

Rochambeau nodded. "Okay, I could do with some myself. I'll order some Chinese." He shut off the recorder.

"I'd rather have Italian," said List.

Rochambeau grinned. "Only one way to settle it, then. Rock, paper, scissors."

List grunted. "You always win at that."

The two detectives beat their right hand into their left palm three times, and shot their choice. List had scissors, but Rochambeau had chosen rock.

"I win again. Chinese it is."

"Doesn't matter," said List. "Nothing does."

Rochambeau got the orders from List and Spenser and used his cell phone to call for takeout. He turned back to Spenser and switched the recorder back on. "So you tried twice, and lost a dog and a bike. What next?"

"Jewelry. I had a femme fatale give him a case of a missing necklace. He'd recover it, return it, and she'd sleep with him. I'd give him the clue, he'd find it, and Bob's your uncle."

"I don't have an uncle," said Rochambeau, his brows knit in a puzzled look.

"It's just an expression!"

"Fine, you don't have to yell. Yeesh."

Spenser studied the detective. "You don't get out much, do you?"

Rochambeau flushed red. "Let's get back to you and the murder."

"So she said she might have lost the necklace at the library. I'd go with him, because I didn't trust him to know where the library even was. I'd leave the necklace for him to find, lead that horse to water and make damn sure he drank it."

Rochambeau started to ask the question, but stopped when he saw the look in Spenser's eye.

"And we'd learned another lesson. The thing was just a cheap piece of costume jewelry, just in case he screwed this one up as well. So off we go. We're in the stacks, and I drop the thing where he's got to practically trip over it."

"And?"

"And he tripped over it. But at least it was in his hands, now, and he could feel like he'd done something. So all we had to do was return to the office and call her. And yet…" Spenser made a sound of disgust.

"How could he possibly mess that up?"

"As we're leaving the library, he starts twirling the necklace on his finger. Before I could stop him, the thing flies off, hits the ground, and slides into a sewer drain. Gone forever."

"Ouch."

"Yeah, so now he's actually questioning whether he's the greatest detective ever, and it's possible he's getting a glimmer of reality. He tells Mommy, and of course she swoops in to fix things. She threatened me again, saying Iggy better get a win and come out on top, or you-know-who was going to be at the bottom. She demanded that I up the stakes, because he'd said the cases he'd got so far hadn't really given him a chance to shine."

List left the room and came back with lunch. They set the cartons out and started eating.

Spenser went on. "I set up a fight scenario, where four guys surrounded and attacked us. I took a dive and went down, then hit Spenser with a tranquilizer dart, and when he woke up, I told him he'd beat up all of them after taking a blow to the head that would have killed most men. Even scuffed his knuckles up and put some fake blood on like he'd punched them out. He was over the moon, even though he didn't remember a thing.

"So for the next set piece, I had him question a supposed Underworld character, 'Big Tony Lucchino' about some rackets they were running. I figured there was no harm, as there were no rackets, because 'Big Tony' was actually Sherman Feldstein, an actor from the Neptune City Playhouse in New Jersey, where he'd just finished a run as Tevye in *Fiddler on the Roof*. What could possibly go wrong?"

"So what went wrong?"

"He went off on his own. He went to *Carmine's*, a well-known restaurant that gangsters frequent, and he fronted Alfredo Parmigiani, a real mobster. Told him he knew of the racket being run with Big Tony, and said he'd better quit and get out of town if he knew what was good for him. Even left our business card, the damn fool. Alfredo didn't do anything with all those witnesses there. But it turns out there is a real Big Tony, and Alfredo sent some of his boys to our office to de-persuade us from sticking our noses in. Of course Iggy wasn't there, so they used me for a pinata.

"Iggy came to visit me in the hospital, and vowed to take down the ones that had done this, even though I pleaded with him not to do anything. He went off and caused enough trouble that Daddy had to step in to save his life by making some arrests of his former business partners. The resulting power vacuum started a mob war, which is why you guys have been so busy lately. All because of him."

Rochambeau snapped off the recorder. "I'm gonna erase that part about the governor being partners with the mob."

Spenser nodded, his face even sadder. "Of course you are. That's how it works."

They'd finished their food, and each man unwrapped a fortune cookie.

Spenser opened his and read his fortune. "*'You will be outsmarted by a fool.'* Well that one's true enough. What's yours say?"

Rochambeau crumpled the small slip of paper and tossed it to the side. "*'You're not as smart as you think you are.'* I think I got yours, Spenser. How about you, List?"

"Mine says '*You are alone in a meaningless universe.'* Figures."

"Man, that's pretty bleak." Spenser shook his head.

"That's life." List shrugged.

"Back to it, then." Rochambeau flicked on the recorder. "Tell us about the murder."

Spenser brushed cookie crumbs from his shirt. "I had one last chance, so I created a rescue script. Our secretary, Velma, would be kidnapped, and Iggy would figure out where she was and save her. For which, of course, she'd fall in love and into bed with him. That would get Mommy off my back, and maybe even Junior would be tired of this game and go on to some other misadventure. Win-win all around."

"I'm guessing it didn't turn out like that."

Spenser gave Rochambeau a long look. "Damn, you are quite the detective."

Rochambeau pursed his lips. "So what did happen?"

"I set the clues up so carefully that even he couldn't fail. Worked like a charm. He tracked each clue and went to the warehouse where Velma was tied up in a chair, with two guys, more actors, guarding her. Iggy would overpower the guys and release Velma. But one of the actors was also an idiot. He was a Method Actor, thus he brought a real gun, so he could get into the role. While he was wrestling with Iggy, the gun fell out. Iggy grabbed it and shot him. The other actor ran out of there faster than a cartoon roadrunner.

"When Mommy's troubleshooters came to straighten things out, even the crooked cops couldn't hide a dead guy that easily. And of course Iggy couldn't be tainted with the brush of even accidental death, so they pinned a murder on me. They promised me that if I confessed, there'd be leniency in sentencing, like only twenty years or so, but I doubt it. They'll never let me out."

Rochambeau shut off the recorder. "Great. Now I have a lot of editing to do. You know I can't use that."

"Wow. I feel so bad for you, having to do all that work to cover up a frame job of an innocent man."

"Know what I think? I think you were jealous of Ignatius, of his connections and money, if not his abilities. So you set this all up to bring him down."

"That what the DA told you to say?"

Rochambeau looked like he'd been caught doing something naughty. "Mostly."

"And you," Spenser said to List. "I suppose you'll go along with this because nothing matters, right?"

List shrugged. "I don't make the rules of the universe."

Spenser rubbed his brow. "So what happens to Iggy now? I guess he's out of the Private Eye game."

Rochambeau looked at List and back at Spenser. "We hear he's considering a run for public office."

The maniacal laugh that followed was the beginning of Spenser's insanity plea.

***

Registry

"I guess you're Alex," the woman said, glancing down at the image on her mobile phone and back up to the man's face.

"That's right. And you must be Cory."

"Yes." She smiled and glanced around. "Are we staying here?"

"We have a table reserved. Unless you'd rather go somewhere else."

"It's a little noisy, but here is fine," she shrugged. "It looks nice."

"These days, all the popular places are noisy," he said. "But the food is really good. It has a four-point-five on Yelp. The Chicken Marengo is to die for."

"Okay then."

Soon they were seated in the dining room, but had no time to take in the view before a pony-tailed waiter with a trim beard and an earring appeared and handed them thick leather-bound menus. He also set down a basket of rolls, the bread wrapped in a crisp white cloth. He introduced himself and offered to take their drink order.

Alex looked at Cory and she smiled, a hesitant sort of thing, as if seeking approval for something slightly naughty. "A glass of the house Chardonnay, please."

"Very good. And you, sir?"

"I'll have the Cabernet."

"I'll go get those and be right back."

They looked at each other and Alex grinned. "So. Alone at last."

"I have a confession," said Cory. "This is my first time using a dating service."

"You look great. It should be easy for you to find someone."

"Not everyone is willing to take it slow these days."

"I hear you," Alex said, leaning forward slightly. "Believe it or not, there's pressure on the guys, too. That's why I'm still single. Waiting for the right one."

"So your profile said you're into finance. What is that, exactly?"

"My father's firm. Does mergers and acquisitions. High-level money deals. It's a lot of pressure."

"Do you like it?"

Alex shrugged. "It's okay. Hard to bail on the family business, so I kind of have to like it, if you know what I mean. But it doesn't leave much time for getting out and meeting nice people."

"The people you work with aren't nice?"

"Only if you like the Gordon Gecko type. All they think about is money, and how to get more of it."

"And here we go," said the waiter as he set down the glasses of wine with a flourish. "Shall I give you a few minutes?"

"Yes. We haven't even looked," said Alex, a touch of annoyance in his voice.

"No problem. I'll be back when you're ready."

Alex shook his head at the departing waiter. "He seems a cheerful sort." He held up his wine glass. "Cheers. To new beginnings."

Cory clinked her glass to his in the toast, and took a sip. "That's good."

Alex grinned. "Are you sure a first-grade teacher should be drinking wine?"

She laughed, hand over her mouth. "If you knew what we went through, you'd be surprised I'm not into the tequila shots by now."

He chuckled. "Kids are tough, huh?"

"Other people's kids are. Especially when they're not taught to behave at home. I don't know what's wrong with some parents. The kids think they can do exactly what they want, and these little tykes even sass me when I gently and politely tell them they can't do something which might hurt someone else."

"Not a lot of money in teaching, for putting up with all that."

"Some things are more important."

"True," Alex said, sipping his wine. "Our firm does a lot of charity work. My way of giving back. It's important to me. I even coach a Little League team. Kids will listen, you know, you just have to keep a firm hand."

"Maybe I should have you come into the classroom."

He smiled. "So let's take a look at what's on offer. Though I already know I'm getting the Chicken Marengo."

"Creature of habit, are you?"

"No, I can be adventurous. But I know that dish will knock my socks off, and I'm in the mood for it. You'd like the shrimp risotto with asparagus. It gets high marks."

"Okay, I'll try it, if you say so." Cory closed her menu and set it down.

Alex smiled and sipped his wine, looking at her over the glass.

The waiter suddenly appeared like a summoned genie popping in. "All set to order?"

They did so, and there was a lag in the conversation before the next topic.

"So what do you like to do for fun?" Alex took out a roll and pulled it apart in preparation for buttering. "When you're not teaching?"

"I like picnics," said Cory. "Just sitting someplace scenic, talking and enjoying the surroundings. How about you?"

"I have a friend who has a sailboat. He lets me take it out sometimes. It's great to be skimming along the waves, riding with the wind."

"That does sound like fun."

"Maybe I could take you out sometime."

"I'd like that."

"No bread for you?"

"I don't want to fill up. And here comes the salad."

The salads were served, and there was another pause as the two ate without talking. Alex took a sip of wine. "Ever want to be anything more than a teacher? Move up to superintendent, anything like that?"

"I don't know. That's a lot of responsibility."

"Schools need good people to run them. You can do a lot of good."

"True. But it's not where my heart lies."

"I guess you'll have to follow your heart, then."

"How about you? What are your plans for advancement?"

Alex shrugged. "I'll probably take over the firm one day, when dad retires."

"Is that what you want?"

"I'd rather buy my own sailboat and spend a lot of time on the water. Maybe sail around the world, like Joshua Slocum."

"Ah, the man who wrote the book on it."

"Top marks, teacher. Most people today have never heard of him."

"I read a lot."

"Did you always want to be a teacher?"

"Guess I did."

Alex pulled apart another roll.

Cory put her fork down. "It's so expensive here. Things were a lot cheaper back in Iowa."

"Have you been here long?"

"Couple of years. How about you?"

"Transplant, like you. Came here from California."

"So your father started a firm here?"

Alex paused to take a sip of wine. "Started it back there, opened a new office here, closer to the New York markets and a better time zone."

They made small talk until the entrees arrived. Cory tried her dish and declared it superb. They chatted amiably as they progressed through the meal, and Alex ordered a second glass of wine, while Cory declined.

The waiter came to take away their dinner plates, and offered them a dessert menu. Cory turned that down as well, saying she was too full to consider anything else. Alex talked her into a coffee, at least. They chatted for a while, lingering over the coffee.

The waiter set down the folder with the bill inside, and Cory casually picked it up and tucked some money inside.

"What are you doing?" Alex looked puzzled.

"Paying my share."

"It's my treat. I insist."

Cory laughed. "Don't be so old fashioned. It's not fair for you to pay for everything, and I can afford dinner, even on a teacher's salary."

"It sounds like you don't want to see me again."

"That's not it at all. Oh, don't look so cross. It means we don't owe each other anything, so we can choose to meet again, with no obligation." She handed the folder over and smiled. He appeared reluctant to give in, his mouth in a tight line.

Soon they got up and left the restaurant. On the sidewalk outside, Cory gave Alex a quick hug. "I had a nice time." She moved towards one of the cabs waiting by the curb.

"I can take you home," he said.

"No need. Call me, though. We can do this again some time."

He frowned as she got in the cab and it pulled away.

Half an hour later, Cory opened her door to see Alex standing there.

She shook her head. "What are you doing?"

He smiled. "I just thought I'd drop by to make sure you got home okay."

"How did you find out where I live?"

"The Internet."

She pulled her robe tighter around her. "Well, I'm okay. Goodnight."

"Aren't you going to invite me in?"

"No."

"Why not? You said you had a good time."

"I did, but this is not appropriate."

"Look, I won't stay long," Alex said. "I just wanted you to know I think you're special. You're not like anyone else."

"Thank you. But you'd better go."

"I will, but just let me make a phone call first. Mine ran out of juice."

Cory frowned and paused, but stood back to let him in.

"Nice place," he said.

"Thank you. The phone's in there."

"Surprised you still have a landline. Lots of people are getting rid of them."

She said nothing, and he picked up a framed photograph.

"Who's this?"

"My sister. You going to make that call?"

"Okay, okay. What's the rush?"

"It's late, and I'm tired."

"Early to bed, early to rise, huh? I get it. Shame you won't offer me a nightcap, though."

"There's nothing to drink."

"Not even a glass of water?"

"Is that what you'd like?"

"Sure."

She went to the kitchen area and took out a glass, then filled it from the faucet.

He was close behind when he spoke. "Not even bottled?"

"You startled me."

"You don't have to be afraid, you know."

She crossed her arms. "I'm not afraid, but I am getting annoyed."

"I'm just trying to be nice."

"Well, it's time for you to go. I need to go to bed."

He took the glass and set it on the counter. "So do I. With you."

"You really need to go. Now."

"I don't think so."

"Get out. Do I have to call the police?"

"We've got a mutual attraction, don't try to deny it." He moved closer and gripped her shoulders.

"Let go of me."

"Look, we can make this fun."

"Or what?"

"You know you want it. You invited me in."

"And now I want you to let go of me, get out now, and leave me alone. For good."

"Aren't you the little tease? Join a dating service, meet someone nice, form an attraction, and then tell him he's not good enough?"

Cory shrieked and struck upward with the palm of her hand under Alex's nose. He cried out as he released her and staggered backward. His hand went to his injured area, coming away with blood.

"You bitch. You broke my nose."

"I told you to let go of me."

"You hurt me. Now I'm going to hurt you."

Two women suddenly appeared, tasers aimed at Alex. "Hands up."

Shocked and uncomprehending, he complied. One woman yanked his hands behind him and snapped on a pair of plastic restraints. Then she led him to a chair and pushed him into it. Cory went to a cupboard and brought out a bottle of tequila. She took out a small glass and poured a generous measure, and set the glass on the table before Alex. The woman behind Alex freed one of his hands, and cuffed the other to the chair.

"You wanted a nightcap, so have one," said Cory.

"Thought you didn't have anything to drink," he said.

"I lied, just like how you lied to force yourself in here when I didn't want you."

"You'd better let me go," he said. "Or you'll be in a lot of trouble."

"You're the one that's in trouble, George," the woman behind Alex said. He stiffened, but forced a grin.

"It's a game, right? Throw a scare into me?"

"Drink up."

"And if I don't?"

The woman showed him a set of pliers with extra-wide jaws. "I use this in an area you will not like."

"You're bluffing."

The woman applied the pliers and squeezed the handle, evoking a scream from Alex.

"What are you doing? Get it off!"

"You going to drink?"

"Yes, you crazy bitch, fine. I'll drink."

He reached out with a shaking hand and took the glass. He downed it in a few gulps.

Cory refilled the glass, and the woman spoke. "Again."

"You trying to get me drunk?"

"Drink."

"Who are you people, anyway?" He took the glass and drank it down, taking pauses now between each swallow.

"People who track people like you."

"Like me?"

"Predators. Oh, look, George, your glass is full. Drink it down."

"My name is Alex." He was pouting, but he took the glass and drank.

"That's what you call yourself now. But before, you were George."

"I'm not that person anymore."

"The only thing that's changed is the name. Not how you prey on women."

"Is that what this is about?"

"What?"

"She was lying."

"Who was, George?"

"That woman. Why I had to leave."

"The glass is full, George."

"I can't drink anymore. I'll get sick."

"That's too bad. This is going to hurt." The plier jaws clacked, as if hungry.

"I'm drinking, don't do it."

"So that woman, George. What did she lie about?"

"What I did to her."

"It's pretty plain what you did."

"She led me on. She wanted it."

"Like Cory here tonight?"

He was silent, watching Cory pour out another measure.

"That's not her real name, is it?"

"No, George, like you, she's free to change it. But she's not running from a court record, like you."

Alex/George was feeling the effects of the tequila. As soon as he would finish the glass, it was refilled. He had lost count of how much he had consumed.

"So I made a mistake. I'm sorry."

"But that wasn't the first time, was it, George? There was that other girl, the one when you were seventeen."

"Those records were sealed."

"Sure, you were underage, and your daddy had money. But word eventually gets out about stuff like that. Especially when the girl you attacked commits suicide."

He smacked the glass down on the table. "So this is about revenge?"

"Oh, no, this is about prevention."

"What?"

"Making sure you don't do this again. Third strike, George. You don't get a fourth."

"So what are you going to do to me?"

"You're going to have a nasty car accident, because you were dead drunk."

"Ah."

"Count yourself lucky. The alternative is to feed you into a wood-chipper, a little at a time, and your disappearance will be just another mystery."

"You're crazy."

"Wonder why we're like that? Maybe because sometimes we just want to meet someone nice, and psychos like you take advantage of us. And when you do, you usually get away with it. So one woman started a special registry. When you moved here, you made the watch list. When you joined the dating service using a fake name, you were flagged for treatment."

"You set me up."

"We didn't make you assault anybody. But we are stopping you from any further assaults."

"You won't get away with this. I know people. Important people."

"You've used up all your people collateral, George. And yes, we will get away with it. We have, hundreds of times. Now don't you wish you'd made different life choices?"

Alex/George started to cry, spending his last few minutes of life in serious regret.

***

Dale T. Phillips

Stranger in Town

If you drove across the Great Plains of America, and happened upon the town of Baronfield in your travels, you might not think there was anything special about it. To the naked eye, it appeared as another collection of weather-beaten, nondescript, grayish, buildings, housing plain, simple country folk, hundreds of miles from any city of note. Some wags joked that the founder, one James Baron, had somehow got lost on his pioneer way, and simply gave up trying to find anything, or that he missed the sea, and was reminded of it by the endlessly flat land that stretched in all directions.

If you were to ask the townspeople of Baronfield what they were most proud of, they would all tell you their pride was one of their residents, young miss Mattie Stark. Many communities have a hometown celebrity who captures their hearts, but Mattie had enraptured the populace so completely, so thoroughly, it was if they were bewitched. Mattie had won the state beauty queen title for unmarried young ladies the year before, and was therefore acknowledged by the townsfolk to be the most attractive person in the entire state. Some would have claimed the entire *country*, even though few of them had traveled outside the town limits, except to attend the pageant when Mattie had won. Still, they were firm in their belief that Mattie outshone any other, the fairest of them all.

Mattie was no mere comely country lass, but a paragon of all that could be said to be attractive. She wasn't like the pale, rosy-cheeked Nordic maids of the states to the north, or the tanned, horsey women of the states west and south, nor the sophisticated, glamorous women of the eastern cities, or even the peachy Southern belles, but something apart from all that and yet somehow more. She had the golden aura of summer itself. If she entered a room, everyone began to smile, and felt that a soft breeze had graced them, bringing the scent of flowers. Children flocked to her as though she were a Pied Piper. All fell in love with her, and other young women could not even find it in their hearts to be jealous. Her voice was pure music, and when she sang, it rang so true and clear and beautiful as to wring tears from the stoniest-hearted listener. She brought light and freshness and joy to all who met her, and Baronfield felt blessed that she was of them.

When she had won the beauty queen title, it confirmed all they had ever believed she was, and they burned with a fierce pride that she was theirs. They were even more proud when she refrained from going on to more beauty queen pageants, saying she was happy to stay right at home. They knew she would have won, and then she might have been entranced by the outside world to leave Baronfield. All they wished for was that she would stay and shine her light upon them for many years to come.

Mattie's father had passed on years before, and when growing up, her mother doted on the girl-child. For years, various establishments in town offered Mattie plum jobs, those hiring her happy just to have her on premises, her duties as light as could be. Townspeople would patronize the business when they knew she was working. At parades and all town functions, she was always guest of honor. And yet she seemed contentedly humble, despite the entreaties of dozens of would-be swains, men young and old who besieged her with offers of marriage, riches, and more. She refused them all, as graciously and gracefully as possible, leaving them despondent that their lives would always be the emptier.

The folk of the town rolled along in a plain existence, content with their place in the world and their treasure. Not very much happened, but that was all to the good, for change was a thing to be feared. But change came one day when a stranger came to town.

The visitor was Nathan Wharton, a man who instantly sparked comment, as he took a room for a week in advance, at the only lodging the town afforded, a motor court for those travelers who might have lost their way, or been stranded in a storm. There was no other room for rent within fifty miles. The gossip mill exploded, and within an hour, almost everyone in town was alerted to the presence of a stranger. Speculation ran rife, and this being a high point of excitement for the week, wagers were even made as to the stranger's origin and business.

The stranger was of a good height, well-built, with sandy hair, pleasant features, and good manners. When he went to dinner that night in the town's only restaurant, the Dine Inn, Glenda, his waitress for the evening, was carefully coached on just how to ask him for the right amount of information without going too far. She was skillful, and a good choice of interrogator, and managed to find out a fair amount.

His name they already knew from the motor court register. The license plate on his expensive car was from California, and he admitted he was from there. And when asked what brought him to this fair burg, he said something that struck terror in their collective hearts, for he was looking for Mattie Stark. He had seen a video of the pageant of the previous year, and of course been struck by the beauty of Mattie. He was a movie producer, and wanted to ask her to fly out to the West Coast for some screen tests. He thought she might have a career in movies.

Panic spread through the town at the news, which flew to all corners before dessert was even served. Should they tell Mattie, or lie and say she had left town, whereabouts unknown. The debate was heated and contentious. A hasty meeting of concerned citizens was convened. The only point of agreement was that the pageant, which had formerly occupied a cherished place in town history, was now thought of as the worst disaster to ever strike the town, including the twister of '38. For it had spread knowledge of her beauty too far.

Three of the town fathers quieted the others when they vowed they would settle the matter, and prevent Mattie from being tempted away.

Later that night, the stranger disappeared from the eyes of men, along with his car and belongings. It was as if he had vanished from the face of the earth. There were sighs of relief when the town realized the problem had been solved. Mattie need never hear of the stranger, and life would go on as usual.

But then the town began to suffer a string of tragedies, as if the heart of it had turned black and withered. An accident at the mill claimed four lives. Three others suffered fatal illnesses in a brief span, and one child ran away. People now whispered, where before they had cheerily greeted each other, and some claimed that a darkness had befallen Baronfield.

The culmination came in the fire that consumed the Stark household one terrible night. Mattie's mother never made it out of the blaze, and Mattie herself barely survived. But she had been badly burned, and her ruined face was twisted and ridged with scar tissue. From a thing of pride, she was now an object of pity.

Some of the townsfolk said it was their just due, that they were paying for their great hidden crime. They had been humbled in their pride, and now endured their sorrow. Mattie lived for many years after, a constant reminder to them of their overweening pride and the wages of sin.

***

Dale T. Phillips

I Know this Town

I saw what happened that night, but I can't tell anybody. I don't know what to do, and I'm scared.

You'll likely think I'm just a kid, that I don't know *anything*, that I made up what I saw. So you'd be like most grownups, who can't be trusted. Even my dad, who I loved, but who said he'd always be around to take care of us. Then he got sick and died, and mom just fell to pieces. So I'm pretty much on my own now. Good thing I can take care of myself. I'm almost eleven years old, and I know this town better than just about anyone.

My name's Pomona. My dad told me she was the Roman goddess of fruit. It's also a city south of us, but I'll stick to the Romans, thank you. I've read stuff about them. Some of what they did was good, but the book said they also kept slaves, so *they* can't be trusted either. Grownups lie a lot, and every time I've told them a secret, I've been punished for it. Like how when Roger broke that new fence, and I told on him. He and his brother found out, and they caught me and beat me up pretty bad. I told on them for *that*, and they beat me up again, so I guess grownups just don't care. One Halloween I told my mom and dad my stomach was hurting, and they said I'd just eaten too much candy. I actually had appendicitis, and almost died before they took me in to the doctor. And when I got my shots for the sickness, the nurse said it wouldn't hurt, but it did. A lot. I don't know why they all lie so much.

We'd almost been ready to go out places after we got our shots, but then there was another wave of people getting sick, including my dad. So mom locked us in, and said it was too dangerous to go out. But I'd been inside for so long that I'd read all my Nancy Drew books twice, and all the others, too. I couldn't take it anymore, and started slipping out at night. If mom knew, she'd have a cow, and say it was way too dangerous. I ride my bike all over and explore the town when it's quiet, and most people aren't around. My bike's a little rusty, but it was my dad's, and it's what he called "retro," because it's got that banana-shaped seat and the big drop handlebars, with long colored plastic streamers hanging from the grips. I think of him every time I ride it.

When I come home at night through the fields, the stars are pretty, and there are so many of them. I've gone through there a million times, but it still makes me happy to stop and enjoy them. My dad and I used to look at them through his telescope, but mom got rid of that after he was gone.

If it's cold out, or raining, I go to the bowling alley sometimes. There's a game room where the kids hang out, so the grownups mostly ignore me. If they only knew! I always check under the Coke machine, and find some change there most days. Once in a while I'll buy some cigarettes out of the other machine, which is around the corner from the desk. I have to be careful, because if someone saw me, I'd get yelled at and wouldn't be able to get them anymore. I don't like smoking much, but when I bring cigarettes to share, I get to hang out with Billy and his friends down by the quarry. He's almost fifteen, and has long hair and plays guitar. His friends smoke, but they ignore me, just like the grownups. I don't care. I only do it to be around him and because grownups say smoking's bad for you, even though *they* do it. I also get some gum when I get cigarettes, to hide the smell so mom doesn't notice.

I don't travel the roads much, because of the cars and the people. They might report a kid out at night. There are plenty of places around to explore, like the old barn that's been about to fall down for years. I heard the men down at the barbershop have bets on when it will happen. They say it's dangerous to go in there, but I've gone in lots of times. I even go down to the train yard and play in the boxcars, and walk along the iron bridge the train uses.

I know this town, and all the places I can go. Even places grownups can't. At home, I'm treated like a kid and can't do anything, but at night, I'm powerful, like a superhero, and can go where I want. Nancy Drew goes where *she* wants, and no one tells her she can't do something. I'd like to be like her when I grow up.

One of the places I go is the construction site where they're putting up new houses.

They've got a big fence and a lot of *No Trespassing* signs, but I know a spot where I can slip in.

Anyway, that's where it happened. I was out there one night, and heard some yelling. I saw two men arguing. I was surprised, because people usually don't come out here at night. They seemed pretty mad, though I couldn't understand what they were fighting about. One man had a bag that looked kind of like my dad's bag for stuff when he'd go to the gym. The other guy I recognized as Mister Wilson. He lives over on Lakeview, just a few streets away from me. Dad used to help me deliver his newspaper, back when I had a route, before people got sick.

Mr. Wilson yelled and pointed to the bag. The man with the bag turned to walk away, and Mr. Wilson took out a gun and shot him. I'd seen stuff like that on TV before, but this was different. Even Nancy Drew hadn't seen people get shot. I didn't know what to do, but I stayed real quiet. I knew if Mr. Wilson heard me, he'd shoot me, too.

The man who'd been shot didn't move. I knew what that meant. He was dead, just like my dad. Mr. Wilson stood next to him and said some bad swear words. He looked around and tucked the gun away. He walked over to a car and started it up and drove the car close to the dead man on the ground. He parked and got out, and opened his car trunk. He said some more swear words as he lifted the dead man up and put him into the car trunk. Then he closed the trunk and picked up the bag. He unzipped it and looked inside. He laughed, but it wasn't the nice kind of laugh, more like Roger when he's being mean. He put the bag in his car and drove away.

I guessed he was going someplace to hide the body, so the police wouldn't catch him. There were lots of places I knew where he could go, but I tried to think of someplace really safe, where other people wouldn't find the body in a million years. Where would I do it?

The quarry. Yeah, that was a good spot. The water was deep, and so cold you couldn't swim in it, except maybe the really hot days in the Summer. And of course he couldn't go out to the place where all the kids hung out, he might get seen by someone. He'd have to go around the point, to that spot that couldn't be seen from anywhere else in the quarry.

I got on my bike and started pedaling for the quarry. His car was faster, but I knew shortcuts. Even so, all I saw was the car coming out by the quarry road, so he must have already pushed the guy in. Maybe he even weighted him down when he did it. I saw that on another TV show. I like watching shows like that, even though mom doesn't approve, because I imagine what Nancy would do.

I rode down near the edge of the quarry, and used my flashlight to look around. I saw the tire tracks from the car, and the ground looked like something had been dragged to the edge. So I knew I was right.

But I couldn't tell anyone, not my mom, not even the police. Grownups couldn't be trusted, and they probably wouldn't even believe me. And I'd seen a TV show where some guy was arrested, but they let him go and he went and killed the person that told on him. I thought that might happen to me, so I'd have to figure something else out. I rode back home and slipped back into my upstairs bedroom without waking mom. But it was a long time before I could fall asleep, because I was pretty scared.

The next day, I found a note from mom saying she was going to the doctor's, and wouldn't be back until after lunch. I thought it might be a good idea to see if I could check out Mr. Wilson's house for clues. Maybe he left the gun there, or that bag he'd taken from the other man.

I rode my bike past his house. He wasn't married, and he lived by himself. His car wasn't in the driveway, so I figured he wasn't home. At the end of the street I pushed my bike down the path by the lake. I left it under some bushes, and cut through backyards, until I was behind Mr. Wilson's house. He had a high fence, so no one could see me there. I went up to the back door and knocked. Nobody answered. It was locked, though, so I checked out his shed, which didn't have a lock. I saw a stepladder, and dragged it over to the house and set it up. I could reach the window in back, and that one wasn't locked. I pushed it up and wiggled my way inside.

This was the kitchen. I have to say, Mr. Wilson wasn't much of a housekeeper. There were dirty dishes all piled up in the sink, and I could smell the trash, which he hadn't taken out, even though today would be trash pickup day on his street. I started looking for clues, trying to keep things as messy as I found them, though I really wanted to clean up a bit.

I didn't find the gun, or the bag, just some dirty sneakers that were kind of black on the sides and bottom. I didn't find a safe, either, like I saw on some TV shows. I remembered another show where the police had searched a house when they thought the owner had done some crime. Maybe Mr. Wilson was afraid they might search his place, and had put the gun and bag somewhere else.

I got back out the window, shut it, and dragged the stepladder back into the shed. I looked for a shovel and found it, but it didn't have fresh dirt on it, like it would have if he'd buried stuff in his yard. I checked around the yard to make sure, but didn't see any place that looked like it had been dug up.

While I was looking, I heard his car pull up in his driveway. Good thing you couldn't see into the backyard from there. I ran out of there pretty fast, believe me, because I could imagine what he'd do if he found me snooping around.

As I rode my bike away, I tried to think of places around town he could hide something. Someplace safe, where people didn't go near. Where would I hide something valuable? The old barn? No, that could fall over at any time, and somebody might find the stuff he hid. Not in any buildings, because there was always the chance that somebody would come by.

I remembered his dirty sneakers. My sneakers always looked like that when I went down to the train yards. It was the cinders, that got black all over whatever you wore on your feet. So someplace along the tracks, where he wouldn't be seen. The iron bridge! You could climb down from the tracks and stash something way up underneath, that would even be protected from the weather. Yeah, that's where I'd do it.

I rode over to the yards, and along the railroad track that led out of town. I walked up to the bridge, and climbed down underneath. I looked and I looked, but I didn't find anything. Maybe I'd been wrong, but I'd check the other side, just to be sure. After I put my ear to the rail to listen for any oncoming trains, I walked along the bridge to the other end. I climbed down and looked up in the small spaces. I didn't see anything at first, but I crawled up to make sure. There it was, the bag I'd seen. It was a good hiding spot. If I hadn't been looking so hard for it, I wouldn't have found it.

I pulled it out and unzipped it. I couldn't believe it— the bag was stuffed with money! Big bundles of it. There had to be thousands, more than I'd ever seen. No wonder Mr. Wilson had wanted to hide it. I zipped it back up and took it back to my bike. It was hard holding the bag all the way home, but I managed. Like I said, I can take care of myself.

What could I do about Mr. Wilson? I could call the police and tell them, but not say who I was. I wouldn't tell them about the money, though, because they'd just take it. Yeah, that would work.

That night, I slipped out and went down to the bowling alley with some quarters in my pocket. The pay phone was at the back end, on an inside wall to keep some of the noise out. I waited until no one was around there, and made my call, using a handkerchief over the mouthpiece to disguise my voice, like I'd seem on another show. I asked for a detective, and said that Mr. Wilson had shot a man, and dropped the body into the quarry, and told him which spot to check. I hung up and hurried home, hoping they'd check out my story.

The next day, the news was all over town. They had questioned Mr. Wilson, and told him they were dragging the quarry for the body. He was so surprised that they seemed to know everything, so he confessed. In the newspaper stories that followed, they'd found the body, but I didn't see anything about the bag of money, so he must not have told them. Maybe he figured he could go get it later, if he could get out of jail. If so, boy, was he going to be surprised!

Though I'd been plenty scared, I was happy with how it turned out. I'd been just like Nancy Drew, and solved the case. I had a bag of money that no one knew about. I didn't know what to do with it, though. But when I get older, I'll make sure that nobody can tell me what to do anymore. Maybe I'll buy the bowling alley and have cigarettes any time I want, and play all the games I want. That could be fun.

All in all, good thing I know the town so well.

***

Summercrime

For the first day of my plum assignment to Robbery/Homicide, I showed up looking and feeling pretty damn good. I had my shiny new shield and Glock, my shiny new suit (bought specially just for this occasion), and my shiny new attitude. Even better, I was being partnered with John Francis Delacorte, a legend on the force. He worked longer and harder than anyone else, and his arrest and conviction rates put everyone else to shame.

Burning with the bright-eyed eagerness of the new guy, I wanted to make a great impression, so I arrived an hour before my shift was to start. Delacorte was already at his desk, going through reports. He looked me up and down.

"Thompson." It was a statement, not a question.

"Yes sir," I refrained from saluting.

"Good thing you're early. Go home and change."

"Excuse me?"

"That's a nice new suit, and you'll be reluctant to get it messed up. The first time I tell you to crawl through a dumpster looking for something a perp dropped, you'll lose your mind. Get a cheap-ass suit, and pack a bag with backup clothes, a towel and shower gear. Our job gets pretty filthy at times. And it's going to be well into the nineties today, so put some extra shirts in. I don't want you smelling like a goat by this afternoon."

"Oh. Okay."

"And lose the dress shoes. You have to run after a perp, you want speed. Get some inexpensive black running shoes, and put a backup pair in the bag. Twenty bucks says you'll step in somebody's blood or worse your first month."

My face burned red, but he wasn't done. "While you're at home, pack a lunch. We don't usually take the time to stop."

I knew better than to protest the loss of our union-mandated lunch breaks. The price of working with the best.

"And one more thing. Bring me back a decent coffee, not this battery acid. Milk, two sugars. I'm easier to deal with when I've had good coffee."

He smiled, not unkindly, and I knew I'd just had my first lesson.

When enough people finally got the vaccines, life began to get back to something like a version of normal for many. Able to mingle with others once more, people flooded the streets, in search of all the things they couldn't get or get to do when things were locked down. When Summer hit, it was like a crowded Mardi Gras every day, with the bars and businesses packed.

Almost everybody got a break except cops. Things were much better for us when people stayed at home, to the point where we had got complacent. The crime rate had plummeted. With a workload finally at a level where we could handle it, we had made improvements to all our systems, had caught up on paperwork, and even had time to go back and solve some cold cases. We went to the gun range and improved our marksmanship. We took online seminars about dealing with a variety of issues we'd never had time for before. We saw our families a lot more, and didn't have to work overtime.

Now that was all gone, and things were tough again. While it was great that people weren't getting sick and dying from that disease, the social disease of crime was roaring back with a vengeance. With the warm Summer weather and everyone out and about, all types of criminal activity exploded. Business was so brisk, I'd been push-promoted to Robbery/Homicide to deal with the tsunami of new cases.

I returned to the station humbled, wearing an old, cheap suit and even older pair of black casual shoes I could run in, carrying a gym bag with a change of clothes, extra dress shirts, and my lunch. I set a large coffee on the edge of his desk. Delacorte stopped typing on his computer and took a sip. He nodded.

"You didn't spit in it, did you?"

I was shocked until I saw his grin.

"You might think I'm a dick, but I actually asked for you to be assigned as my partner."

"You did?"

"You've got a good record so far, and you're not married. You don't seem to mind going the extra mile, working overtime without clocking it. I've burned out all my partners, the last ones I could count on. Cops who've been on the job for a time want to cut corners, skimp on paperwork, court appearances, knocking on doors. They can't wait to get home at the end of the day. Me, I want to catch every sonofabitch stickup man in the city, no matter how long it takes. Like I said, we work through lunch, and sometimes dinner. You young guys are so damned eager to prove yourself, you'll go along with it for a while before it gets to you. You haven't had time to form any bad habits yet, and you'll listen and learn. So welcome aboard."

He didn't offer his hand to shake, but I was okay with that. I'd seemed to finally pass muster, and I was over the moon. Requested to work with the best.

When we got our vehicle, I was surprised when he handed me the keys. Most senior partners liked to drive. Not Delacorte, he went through files as we motored through the city to our first stop, a bodega that had been held up the day before.

"Didn't someone already get assigned to this?" Since we had our own caseload that we were responsible for, I wondered why we were here.

"Yeah, Carter and Woolsey are the primaries. But they're not as thorough as us. They'll tell a vic to come down to the station and look through mug shots. People here, they don't like cops, and won't usually go to a station. Plus the fact they'd lose half a day of work, which they can't afford. They appreciate when we come back and act like we give a shit. So I bring my own book." He tapped a thick folder.

"You can't have every mug shot in that."

"Don't need them all, I keep my own separate books for separate types of stickups. Around here, four other bodegas have been held up in the last two weeks, same MO. I've got pics of some likely candidates, and a few fakes, to keep down the false positives. And I've got the sketch artist copies from the last four witness IDs.

"It's a damn site harder with so many people wearing masks. And gloves, so we don't get as many prints. People don't look twice at someone entering a business wearing a mask. Since places have a cash flow again, armed holdups are all the rage. A mask gives the robber a few extra seconds before the proprietor knows they're being robbed. Except for banks, that's often enough to do the deed and get away clean."

I'd found a parking spot, but left the engine running to keep the AC on. It was already getting steamy, and the day had just begun. "What about banks? Someone said you don't handle bank jobs."

"Every other swinging dick wants to handle the bank jobs, because they're the glory, and good for getting your picture in the paper. But with the high-tech cameras, alarms, security guards, dye packs and marked bills, bank robbers are really up against it. Plus, it's a Federal crime in most cases, so the FBI swoops in with their labs and analysis and huge resources to build a rock-solid case. The staff at banks are carefully coached to just give up the money, since everything is insured and no one needs to get hurt. It's dangerous to resist, and they know the robber usually doesn't get far. Whatever money the crook gets, often just a few grand, doesn't even pay enough for a good attorney when they come to trial.

"Small-time business stickups are mean and dirty, and a hell of a lot harder to close. The owners don't want to give up their hard-earned cash, so they resist. One of them got killed last week. While most bank robbers are stopped after one or two, the small-time hitters do it again and again, causing a lot more pain. So that's why we're here, on someone else's case. Because I'll bet it's the same punk who hit all these places, and I want him stopped before he shoots someone else, no matter who gets the credit. If that puts us behind on our cases, that's why we miss meals to catch up. You on board with that?"

Of course I was, inordinately proud to be on the team. We went in to the bodega, and the man behind the counter had a bandage on his face, having been pistol-whipped in the course of the holdup. I figured he was lucky not to have been shot. Delacorte greeted the man in Spanish, and held a brief conversation. The man nodded, and they stepped to the side to go through the mug book. After a few minutes, Delacorte thanked the man and nodded to me as we departed.

"Similar description, like I thought," Delacorte said back in the car. "We've got three good candidate sketches, and a Christmas present. The punk wore long sleeves, which Jorge thought was odd, it being so hot. Lots of junkies don't want the world to know, though, so it's not totally uncommon. But when the punk hit Jorge, some of his wrist showed, and he had a snake tattoo. Any of our candidates has one, we've got him."

"Won't Carter and Woolsey follow up on that?"

"They might, but they've got to ID him first, unless the guy is already recorded in our tattoo files. By the time they get around to it, he could hit more places. I don't want to wait. He's already killed once."

"Okay, where to?"

Delacorte was already tapping out a number on his cell. "Snitch City. Under the overpass, over by the park."

"Where all the bums hang out?"

"Punks like to roll them for easy cash. Small risk, because the vics don't go to us afterward. Maybe one of the guys there has seen someone fitting the descriptions." Delacorte spoke into his phone. "Hey, Hector, I'd like a dozen of the usual to go." Delacorte looked at me. "You want a sub? They're good."

"I thought we didn't stop for lunch."

"We don't. But I'm already getting them, so just checking. "

"I brought my lunch, like you said."

"Good man." He spoke into the phone. "Yeah, that's it. Be there soon."

"You buy subs for the bums?"

Delacorte looked at me. "They're human beings, and they usually go hungry. Some are vets, some just got to where they are by bad luck or bad choices. You give them money, they don't buy food with it. So yeah, I feed them, and once in a while they help me out with a tip. They get around the city a lot, and nobody pays attention to them. Sometimes they see stuff that can help."

I filed all that away, and told myself to refer to them differently in the future.

"There's a copy shop after the next light. Pull in."

Minutes later, Delacorte came out with a stack of flyers with facial sketches. I knew how unreliable even eyewitness reports could be, but Delacorte had narrowed down the choices to three candidates. He directed me to the sandwich shop, handed me some money, and I went in to pick up the order.

"Are you Hector? I'm picking up for Delacorte."

The man smiled and put several bags on the counter top. "You his new partner?"

"First day."

"You're lucky, you'll learn a lot."

"How do you know him?"

Hector's face darkened. "We were robbed, two years ago. They shot me. He worked night and day, and got them. He knew how badly my business would be hurting, and started ordering all the time, and overpaying. It's kept us going. The man is a saint."

Back at the car, I put the bags in the back and got behind the wheel.

"Hector's quite a fan."

"He's a man trying to make an honest living, and didn't deserve what happened to him. They almost killed him. So I help out when I can. Besides, he makes a damn good sandwich."

I parked by the underpass, and followed Delacorte, carrying the lunch bags. He approached the men one at a time, handed them a sandwich, and had them look at the sketches. It took about an hour, but we had two people say they'd seen someone kind of like one sketch in the neighborhood a few streets over, by the tracks. The heat was brutal, and I wondered how these poor people withstood it. Both Delacorte and I put on fresh shirts after toweling off.

We drove to the other neighborhood, and split up to go door-to-door with sketches in hand. Delacorte had warned me to watch for sudden changes in demeanor if people recognized the sketch as someone they knew. The guy might have friends who would warn him.

It was needle-in-a-haystack time, and we spent hours knocking on doors and dealing with people short-tempered from the heat. By the afternoon, I was exhausted and drained, and looked as wiped out as I felt. Some people were sympathetic, even offering me cool drinks. But I came up empty every time.

Sometime about four o'clock, Delacorte came up to me, flushed and talking fast. "We got a possible, guy who lives at 404, they said he's got a snake tattoo. Let's go get our vests on."

We went back to the car and called in a request for backup, then removed our suit jackets and put on bulletproof vests over our sopping shirts. We checked our service weapons, and my heart rate was *barrupping* like a jackhammer. A patrol unit pulled up, and Delacorte instructed the two uniforms to go around the back of the building in case we got a runner. Then we climbed four flights of stairs, the air oppressive and still. There was the smell of cooked onions and garbage that almost made me gag.

Delacorte stood to the side of the door, and I remembered training, which said to never knock while standing in the normal spot when someone might shoot.

A voice answered from within, and Delacorte spoke. "City. We're investigating power outages. Some people are running air conditioners and blowing fuses for the building."

"I don't got no air conditioner."

"Excellent, sir, but we have to verify that. If you just open the door, we'll take a quick look and check you off so that no one else bothers you about this."

There was some grumbling as a chain was removed and a lock was opened. As the door swung open, Delacorte charged it, pushing the guy back, with a gun in his face. "Police! On your knees and don't move your hands!"

The guy complied, and Delacorte nodded his head to me. "Clear the other rooms."

Gun held in my sweaty paw, I did so, and luckily saw no one else. I came back out. Delacorte had the guy face down on the rug and was cuffing him. He smiled at me and held up what looked like a 32-caliber, five-shot revolver with taped grips. "Look what he tried to use on me."

"I didn't," the guy yelled. "It ain't mine. He put that in my hand."

Delacorte laughed. "And I suppose this tattoo isn't yours either." He showed me the snake coiled around the guy's wrist. We had our robber.

Later, back at the station, we were filling out the report after getting the guy booked and in a holding cell. Other detectives came by to congratulate us. Even the captain showed up. "Nice work, Delacorte."

"Thank you, sir. The new guy did great."

The captain eyed me with what looked like skepticism, then drilled his gaze into Delacorte. "Was that your case?"

"Not specifically, sir, but we got a good lead, and knew about the other robberies. We ran it down, and got lucky."

"Hmm. Well, make sure your own cases get some attention tomorrow."

Delacorte tipped his head at me after the Captain left. "See? Procedure's more important that catching these guys and stopping them." He handed me a report. "I wrote it up, if you want to take a look and sign it."

I read the report, my brows knit as I saw some discrepancies. And then there was the gun. Had Delacorte planted a throwdown piece on the guy? I looked up at him, the question in my eyes.

He nodded. "Maybe I embellished a little. We have to. The D.A. is a real weak-ass, won't push cases that he can't win in a lock. He's known as 'Plea-bargain Marvin.' He's notorious for knocking down hard felonies to misdemeanors, as long as they plead guilty to something. This guy's new to the game, doesn't have a sheet yet, so unless we get something concrete, he might even walk. The guy wore a mask. If the witnesses can't positively ID him in a lineup, we're screwed. We searched his place, didn't find anything else but the tattoo to tie him to one robbery. He might get tried on only one count, and the judge could go easy, since he doesn't yet have a record. With all the overcrowding, the guy could be out in a year or two. And he'd be right back to holdups. So it's a good thing he had the gun. Means he'll do at least five years, and won't be out in that time to kill anyone else. In our job, it's follow the rules to the letter, which lets the bad guys run amok, or try for some measure of justice. Up to you to decide what's better."

I thought about his words, and saw the truth in them. I convinced myself it was better to go along, and bend the rules for the greater good. If I balked on agreeing to the doctored report, my career was already over, and worse yet, the guy might go free. I signed the report, telling myself it was for the right reasons, but knew I'd already crossed a line.

We worked other cases, slogging through the interminable heat, knocking on hundreds of doors for interviews, day after day. I felt more like a census taker than a cop. The second week on the job, I fulfilled Delacorte's prophesy and stepped backward into a lake of victim blood on a crime scene. I took a lot of heat for that one.

One late night at the station, I was yawning while finishing another long day. Detective Carter grinned at me.

"So how do you like working with Delacorte, newbie?"

"Long hours," I admitted. "What the hell drives him, anyway?

Carter dropped his jocular manner. "He was just like the rest of us. Then his sister was killed in a gas station holdup, along with the clerk. They never caught the guy. Delacorte changed.

He's possessed, and will try anything, hypnosis on witnesses, even a psychic. We laugh, even though he closes more cases than any of us. But he doesn't joke or hang out with us like he used to. He's become the angel of vengeance."

I thought a lot about that, especially later. Because three weeks in, we arrived at a crime scene at a car wash. Somebody had robbed the place for a lousy two hundred and twelve dollars, and tried to grab a car for a getaway. The woman in the car had a gun, and was shot and pulled from the vehicle. She never even made it into the ambulance. Delacorte stood over her body for a long time, his lips moving in silent promise. He took a picture on his phone.

Later in the car, he turned to me. "We've going to catch this guy, no matter what it takes."

My stomach churned at this pronouncement, and I didn't know how far I would go. I didn't have time to think about it in the full-court press of potential witness interviews that followed. Despite our efforts, and a critical lack of sleep, we came up empty. No other locals had tried holding up car washes, so Delacorte scoured national crime reports. He finally found a similar case in Texas, where a guy named Loflin had robbed a car wash and then shot another man, also armed, during a carjacking afterward. There were some irregularities in the case, and the robber only did two years before he got released on parole.

Delacorte was relentless in tracking the man, who seemed to have vanished from Texas. Due to some glitch in their system, they hadn't even issued a warrant for his arrest, despite his having broken parole. Delacorte had hundreds of flyers made with this guy's mug shot plastered on them, and we hit the streets, after Delacorte gave a copy to every patrol officer and detective. We went to Snitch City. We talked to every Confidential Informant we could, every civilian. We staked out car washes, but he didn't hit again. He'd probably gone to ground after the killing, knowing there would be heat.

In defiance of the long odds, we finally got a possible ID on a guy living on the west side of the city. Delacorte and I went to the address. He hadn't called for backup, and I had a bad feeling in my gut, even more so when Delacorte had me go around to the back.

I crept along the back alley, Glock in hand, my guts churning. I thought I had sweated everything out, but my shirt was soaked again, and my hand trembled. I damn near fainted when I heard a voice behind me.

"Don't move, or you're dead, pig."

I froze.

"Drop the gun and put your hands up."

Even with a bulletproof vest on, I didn't have much of a chance. I did as the voice commanded.

"Good thing I was taking out the trash," he said. "How the hell did you find me?"

I couldn't talk, my mouth was so dry.

"What's the matter? Never been shot before?" He laughed. "You'll be my second cop."

"Why?" I managed to croak it out.

"Why what? Stickups? For the money, stupid. And if someone gets in my way, they go down."

"She had two kids."

"The broad? So what? She also had a gun. Bad things happen. Like for you." He chuckled. "Any last words, dumbass?"

"Freeze." Delacorte's voice was the sweetest sound I'd ever heard. "Put the gun down."

"Not happening, pig. I've got the drop on this guy, and I'll shoot him unless you back off."

"You'll shoot him anyway, and the second you do, I'll splatter your brains all over this alley. These are your last seconds on earth, unless you give it up now and spin the justice wheel. Hell, you beat the system once before."

The next few seconds were the longest of my life.

"Good point. Okay, I give up. I'm putting it down…"

The two shots almost made me lose all control. I spun around, and saw Loflin with a surprised look as he fell, two red holes in him, one in the forehead, one in the throat. His gun was already on the ground.

I looked at Delacorte. "Thank you."

"He started to put it down, then tried to shoot. You okay?"

"Yeah, I think so. Might need new underwear."

Delacorte laughed. "We got him, partner. A righteous shoot. One more killer off the streets."

Later, I wasn't so sure. Had Loflin really tried to shoot, or had he truly given up? And did it really matter to me, as much as it would have before, even just a few weeks? What kind of cop was I going to be, one who just followed the rules and let the bad guys continue to hurt innocent people, or one who made sure to stop the crooks who caused so much pain? I still believed in the system, just maybe not as much as I used to.

But I signed the report and walked out of the station, into the simmering heat and endless crimes of Summer.

***

Dale T. Phillips

The Glass Monkey

It was a small thing, just a little monkey figurine made of blue glass, yet it always cheered Beth up to look at it. The smile on the figure was so comical, she couldn't help but smile herself. And it warmed her heart, because it had been given to her when she was only nine, when she still had a fondness that bordered on obsession for all things monkey-related. Her older sister Jane had indulged her passion, and presented her with the trinket that Jane had picked up in some shop on one of her travels. She even called Beth her little monkey, and they had a special bond, as they were not close in years.

Now that Jane was gone, Beth loved the monkey even more as a reminder of her sister's love. She had named it Clarence, and even talked to it in the dark days after her parents had died in the accident, and Jane had not yet arrived to take care of her and arrange matters. It seemed that the glass monkey was all she had left, apart from the money left by her departed parents and sister. And even that was dwindling fast, for Beth's husband Jared did not prefer to work. She often wondered if money was the reason he had married her, for he was good-looking and had a certain charm, while she was plain-featured and an introvert. Jane had warned her against marrying the man, but Beth was elated that he had chosen her as a bride.

Beth tried hard to make him happy, but Jared was difficult to please. He tended to criticize her if things were not exactly the way he liked them. She knew she could not do the things he liked in the bedroom as well, and she suspected he was going elsewhere for his desires. It saddened her, but she soldiered on and did not bring it up.

The one thing she did refuse to budge on was selling the house. It had been in her family for generations, and she had been raised in it, and did not want to part with the memories. Certainly it needed repairs, but Jared merely saw it as a falling-down old structure that they could make a tidy profit from, and he constantly importuned her that they should move to some warmer climate. His insistence grew stronger as the bank account shrank. Beth herself wondered what they would do when all the money was gone, but she didn't like to think too deeply on it.

Luckily, the accounts from the trust were still in her name, or the money would have been gone long before. From time to time, Jared would bring up some moneymaking scheme he'd heard about, and see if he could convince her to withdraw more funds to give to him to allow him to participate. Her steadfast refusals were a source of tension between them. Deep in her heart she had to admit that if she gave him the money it would vanish almost overnight, for Jared was not someone who handled finances well.

Take, for example, the subject of life insurance. Jared had wheedled her for some time to pay extra for the policy of a half-million dollars, a sum she found excessive. In the end, he had won, and Beth paid for something she hardly felt she needed, but of course it was for Jared's sake, not for hers. There was no one else in the family to inherit anything, and Jared said he had no other family, that each other was all they had.

It would have been enough for Beth, but Jared had begun to drink more, and his temper flared more than usual. He was surlier, and without the charm he put on when he wanted to, he was downright disagreeable. Beth walked on eggshells much of the time, not wanting to set him off. She did not bring up unpleasant subjects, and strove to placate him when he was in one of his moods. She would have liked a companion and had wanted a cat as a pet, but Jared had vehemently vetoed that, saying he would not put up with an animal that needed taking care of, as he had enough to do. Beth wondered what that might be, as most of what he did was sit on her couch and drink.

Growing ever more distant from Jared, Beth began once more to talk to her little glass monkey, her oldest and dearest friend. She rarely went out, and saw very few people. She had no social circle, so good conversation was hard to come by. Jared was morose when he wasn't drinking, and conversation had never been his strong suit. The days were long and mostly silent, when Jared wasn't having one of his ever-more frequent tantrums.

His latest bête noire was the rowboat he had insisted on buying. A small river ran behind the big New England Victorian, and Jared had mounted a campaign to convince her they need a rowboat for recreation. Beth had agreed to the boat, but would not go out on the water with him. He had badgered her for over a week, and today she had told him she wanted to hear no more of it, as she would not go. So he had gone to his old friend the bottle while he built up a good head of steam. She wondered why it mattered so to him.

Late in the afternoon, Jared tried again to get Beth to join him out on the water. When she told him he was in no shape for that sort of thing, having put away most of a bottle of bourbon, he began to curse. When he broke a bowl on the coffee table, Beth cried out, and this seemed to stoke his rage. He picked up one of the plants and hurled it against the far wall. Regrettably, this was where Clarence sat on his shelf. When she cried out and went to the mess that had been made, she saw the glass bauble now in two pieces, the head broken off.

The loss she felt was for more than just a figurine, and it cut deeply. She wept, and Jared raged on, swearing and hurling insults at her back. She closed her eyes and wondered why she continued to put up with this. Perhaps she didn't have to. She would tell him to leave, to just go. She picked aimlessly at the mess, the plant which had burst from the broken pot, scattering dirt all about, the collapsed shelf, the decapitated glass monkey. She put the two pieces of glass in her pocket. She closed her hand around a large shard of the pot.

Beth stood up and turned to Jared.

"What?" The sneer on his face strengthened her resolve. His contempt had become too much to bear.

"You have to go. Leave now."

His mouth hung open in disbelief. "What do you mean?"

"I've had enough. You're no good, and you have to go."

"I'm your husband. I'm not going anywhere."

"This is my house, my home, and I want you to get out of here and never come back. Take your things and go."

Jared stood up, eyes red, unsteady on his feet. He was even more inebriated than usual. "This isn't funny."

"It's not meant to be."

"You can't talk to me that way."

"First time for everything."

"It's because I broke the shelf? Or that stupid monkey?"

"It's because you broke my heart."

Jared glowered at her, and a sly smile came over his face. "Maybe it's time to collect on that insurance."

She cocked her head. "What do you mean?"

"Time to take a ride in the rowboat, Beth." He giggled.

Her head spun. Was he really that far gone? Was that why he had increased the insurance, so he could drown her and claim it was an accident? Her blood chilled. Good thing she hadn't given in and gone out with him.

He lunged for her, arms outstretched. She swung her arm up to protect herself, and the jagged tip of the pot she held pierced Jared's throat as he impaled himself. Beth stepped back and saw Jared claw at the slice of glazed clay lodged in his windpipe, blood seeping around the edges. He took three staggering steps and fell face down into the mess he had caused. He shuddered once and lay still, and Beth stared, unbelieving, her breathing ragged. Everything had changed in the course of a few minutes.

Jared did not move, and Beth put two fingers to the side of his neck, careful not to dip them in blood. She felt no pulse. She ran to the bathroom and took out the small hand mirror and brought it back. She tilted Jared's head to the side and held the mirror before his open mouth. No misting at all. Dead for certain.

Well. Should she call someone? The police? She didn't like the thought. They might think she had deliberately done this and put her on trial. No, she didn't want that. But what should she do? Bury him somewhere? No, that wouldn't work. She couldn't see herself cutting him up into small pieces, either.

What about the rowboat? She could put him in it and push him downstream. About a mile down the river was some rough water. It would likely upset the boat, and he would spill out. When they found him, it could easily look like an accident.

Beth went to the cellar and brought up a blue plastic tarp. She laid it on the floor next to Jared and rolled him onto it. Then she dragged the laden tarp out the back door, onto the lawn, and down to the bank of the river. It wasn't easy, but she was highly motivated.

The rowboat was there, and she puffed with exertion as she wrenched him into the boat, and hung him over the back, arms in the water. With his throat over the stern and not in the boat, she removed the shard of pottery from his body. She untied the boat and gave it a shove, watching the current move the craft along.

She watched until the boat was gone from sight, her fingers clenched around the broken glass monkey. She wasn't sure what life would be like from now on, but just maybe that insurance money would come in handy now.

***

Dale T. Phillips

Win Win

Janice knew she was in the worst trouble of her life, and her choices were limited. She could let her sister Marie die, or she could stake her own life to make a deal with her local crime boss, Rocky the Dog. But dealing with Rocky was like dealing with the Devil. There was always a catch, and you wound up paying a lot more than you'd bargained for.

Even worse, Janice and Rocky had a history. A few years before, one of Rocky's dealers had sold Janice's sister some smack, and Janice had fought back. She'd started making her own home documentary, filming a dozen of Rocky's top sellers making drug deals before hitting the jackpot. She recorded two of Rocky's lieutenants killing a rival dealer, and even got them saying Rocky's name while doing it. Even with the cops he'd bought off, this would bring him down.

Armed with this, she'd arranged to meet with Rocky to cut her own deal. She'd agree to withhold the video if he told his people to stop selling anything to her sister. Since Rocky ran all the drugs in town, this meant Marie was shut off and could get clean. But it meant Janice would have to sit down and bargain with the most dangerous man in the state.

Janice was in a cold sweat thinking about that first meeting. Rocky had got his name and reputation from raising savage dogs to fight. He had several breeds, and made money arranging contests for men who got their jollies from seeing two beasts maul and try to kill each other. Janice supposed they'd have used people in the fights, if they could have got away with it. Maybe they had.

But about four years back, one of Rocky's dogs had gone berserk from its beatings and mistreatment, and had turned on Rocky, tearing his right hand apart. A stunned Rocky lost his taste for animal breeding and dogfights, but his nickname still stuck, and was only spoken around town in whispers by anyone who wished to keep their health.

For a new business model, Rocky had gone heavily into the drug trade, and within fourteen months had locked up all the trafficking in that part of Massachusetts. In that business, one had to be ruthless, and Rocky excelled at that trait. The ways in which he'd dispatched rivals were the stuff of legend, and quite effective in instilling fear and obedience. It was taken as gospel that no one ever crossed him and lived long enough to enjoy it.

Rocky the Dog's place of business was a back booth in a Chinese restaurant, and Janice knew Nancy, the niece of the owner. Nancy had said they hated that Rocky used them as a business office, but they had no choice. He'd make them open at all hours, and they had to be ready to supply him with whatever food and booze he wanted, whenever he wanted. Their lives had gone to hell since he'd taken over, but there was no escape.

In that first meeting, Janice had sat across from Rocky, as two armed bodyguards stood several feet behind her on either side, impassive as stone idols. Janice had tried to meet Rocky's gaze and shuddered. His eyes were as black and pitiless as those of a snake, with no human empathy in them. She remembered everything, how terrified she was, yet how determined. If he wanted money, her body, anything, she was prepared to do it for Marie.

Rocky the Dog was of medium height, built as solid as a tank, with thick, powerful forearms, and a face pitted with the old marks of bad acne. One long, red-lined scar ran from his forehead down to his ear, and she supposed he loved it, adding to his fearsome look and mystique. He wore a loose, flowing red shirt, with a gold neck chain and enough chest hair showing to confirm his masculinity. He completed the look with a gold earring, like some sort of modern-day pirate, which of course he was. But he kept his damaged hand out of sight under the table, and she wondered if he was ashamed of it.

His voice had sounded like someone had once taken sandpaper to it. But he talked softly, forcing people to lean in and listen carefully.

He'd smiled at her, exposing the glimmer of a gold tooth. "You got a lotta guts, coming to me like this. You know what I can do to people."

Janice, who had practiced for this, had forced a note of humbleness in her voice, though she'd grown up in this tough town, and was anything but humble or obsequious. She was also careful to mask the contempt she felt for this pile of human scum. Tough guys saving face meant everything in this town.

"Everyone knows you're the king here, and can do what you want. I'm not asking for much. Marie is all I have, and I just want a chance to get her clean. She's all I have left. I have to protect her."

Rocky had nodded. "You want to protect what's yours. I respect that." He leaned closer. "But you shouldn't have tried to squeeze my balls. I don't like that. We both know I can get you and your sister into a room, and do things to her that would make you turn that video over to me in less than five minutes."

Janice had felt a river of ice go down her spine, and she waited, her face stiff.

"Got anything to say about that?"

She paused, breathing deeply. "I didn't expect you to do a favor for nothing. I have no money, nothing else to offer you. I needed some kind of leverage for negotiation."

Rocky had sat back and studied her, sucking his teeth. The silence and the pause was torture for her.

"Good point. You tried, kid. You got smarts along with guts, more than a lot of the clowns that work for me. I could use someone like you in my organization."

Janice was gobsmacked. She had come here to *threaten* him, and now he was offering her a *job*?

"Whaddya think?"

Janice stammered. "Thank you, sir, that's flattering, but I don't have what it takes to be in your world."

Once more, Rocky studied her closely, and finally nodded. "Maybe not. It's damn tough out there. Shame, though. You could have done well."

He took a sip from a glass before him. "I like your style. Tell you what. I'm feeling generous today, gonna give you what you ask for. As of this moment, your sister won't even be able to score some weed off a high school kid. She's shut off."

Janice bobbed her head. "Thank you."

"Just don't go aroun' telling people you got one over on Rocky the Dog. I'm giving this to you, but I don't have to, unnerstan'? And I don't want a line of people comin' up askin' me for favors."

"I get it. This ends here."

"Good. Then it's a win-win. Go clean your sister up."

And Janice had. She had got Marie into rehab, and worked her tail off doing three jobs to pay for it. It had seemed to work, up until a week ago, when Marie had relapsed and moved in with a dealer. Janice had been crushed, and wondered how she could break Marie away once more.

So she had to go crawling back to Rocky the Dog, and this time with no leverage. She spent the night before the meeting praying, and steeling herself for whatever she would have to endure.

Rocky had aged a bit in the last two years, she noticed, and had added about twenty pounds. His bodyguard took his time frisking Janice too closely, touching her in places she would have slapped him for if lives hadn't been on the line. A smiling Rocky watched her humiliation, and she swallowed this down and accepted it as part of the price.

"So you're back. Little Sister couldn't stay clean, huh?"

"She moved in with one of your people. Bruno."

"Bruno. Good man. Makes a lot of money for me. I like to keep my people happy when they're making me money. And she's there of her own free will. So now you want me to go make him unhappy, take away something he likes?"

She said nothing, holding back tears by sheer will.

"At least this time you didn't try to squeeze my balls. You learned. Smart, like I said. So you know you got no leverage, but you want another favor."

He swirled the liquid in his glass around before taking a gulp.

"Nothing?"

Janice tried to swallow, but there was a hard knot in her throat. "You once thought I might work for you."

Rocky laughed. "And there it is. Whoa, how things change. What is it you think you could do for me?"

"Whatever it takes." She knew how awful this was, and waited.

"Uh-huh. You were right, though, before, you don't have what it takes to be in my business. You wouldn't last a week."

She sat, waiting, knowing he had something in mind, but wanting to toy with her. He'd known she would come to him like this.

"You're a fine-looking lady. I could put you on the street with my other girls. But you'd just wind up killing a john some night. Bad for business. Nah, can't have that."

He took another drink. "I might have an errand you could do for me. A delivery. Pretty dangerous, though."

"I'll do it."

Rocky smiled. "Good attitude. I like that."

Again she waited. Rocky brought forth a cell phone and activated it. On the screen was the image of a boat, a nice cabin cruiser.

"See this boat? It's owned by one of my competitors. I need to deliver him a personal message. Trouble is, I can't send any of my guys, because, you know. But you, I bet he'd let you on board."

"That's it?"

"Yeah, but the trouble is, he ain't gonna like the message. He might get mad. Real mad. No idea what he'll do to the messenger, get me?"

Janice nodded.

"So there it is. You still game?"

"Of course."

"Good girl. Tonight Bruno will drop your sister off at your place. They're done. Tomorrow at noon, you come back here and pick up a package. You drive straight out to the Danversport Yacht Club, go to this boat, and tell him you've got a message for him."

"What if he won't see me?"

"That's the hard part. You gotta make him see you. You're a smart girl, you'll figure out a way. And I want you to film him, and send me the video, real-time on this phone. I wanna see his face when he opens the package."

Janice smelled something fishy, but kept her poker face. "And we're square after that?"

He smiled. "Until the next time."

Janice knew there would be no next time. If she survived this, she would take Marie and get her the hell away from here and gone. Maybe Montana, or some place like that, where Marie couldn't score, and where there weren't any neighborhood homicidal gangster crime lords. But how was she going to get this delivery done?

That afternoon, Janice ran through various schemes to get on board the boat. *Strip-o-gram? Fruit basket? Party girl in a bikini, with cooler?* Nothing she could come up with seemed a sure thing. She doubted she could just walk up and say she had a delivery from a guy that wanted the boat owner dead. One suspicious drug boss to another.

She began to think about what the delivery was. That was key. She'd first assumed it would be body parts, a warning to the guy about what awaited him. But the more she thought about it, the more she doubted it. If it was, she was dead anyway, because the guy would never let her leave the boat. He'd chop her up and send her pieces back to the guy who had sent her. That's the way these guys did business.

Rocky would want more than just a meaningless warning, which could be sent any number of ways. He didn't do things half-assed, he'd want to send a real message. So maybe the scumbag would give her a bomb, set to blow when the guy opened it, or even operated remotely, from a signal sent to the phone she was filming on. That was why he wanted her to stay there and film it, to assure the guy all was okay. A suicide mission, either way. Solve all of Rocky's problems, while he had a good laugh. And then he could scoop Marie back up and return her to her dealer boyfriend. Win-win.

She knew how to make sure. Her friend Trent worked at a funeral home, and they had an X-ray machine to check bodies for anything before being cremated or buried. He'd be able to scan the package they gave her, no problem. But so what? Even if she knew she was delivering a bomb, it had to go off the way Rocky the Dog wanted, or she and Marie would be dead anyway.

But what if she could hoist Rocky on his own petard? Her friend Nancy had said how they hated having him in the restaurant as a fixture. Would they be willing to blow up a part of the restaurant to get rid of him? She bet they would. Insurance would let them rebuild, as long as Rocky was out of their lives.

She called Nancy, and met her a block from the restaurant. She explained the whole deal.

Nancy listened closely, but shook her head. "They'd get back at us, assuming we'd helped set it up."

Janice grimaced. "Damn. Well, it was worth a shot."

Nancy looked pensive. "Unless…"

"What?"

"If it costs us, too, then they won't be as suspicious. We need a sacrifice."

Janice got it. "Nancy, no. You can't."

"It's family. I'd do it, if I had to, to save the rest of my family. But my uncle has cancer, is in a lot of pain. They've told him it's just a matter of weeks. He's already talked about killing himself. This way, he can be a hero. I think he'll do it. He hates those guys."

Janice stared at her. "I can't imagine doing that for your family."

"The hell you can't. You're willing to die for Marie. How's that any different?"

The next day, Janice drove to the restaurant and took delivery of a Mike's pastry box from the unsmiling goon, who told her not to tamper with it. She knew it didn't contain delicious pastries from Boston's North End, as it was heavier, and much more securely wrapped.

She drove to the funeral home, where Trent carefully put the package on the platform surface and scanned it.

"Jesus, you were right. I wouldn't move that around a lot."

"I don't plan to."

"Do I want to know any more?"

"Don't read the papers unless you do."

From there, Janice drove to the restaurant, where she put the package into Nancy's hands.

Nancy was crying. "He'll do it. The guy's in there, like always. God, I hope we pull this off."

"I'm so sorry, hon. Be safe."

"You too. Get the hell away from here."

From three blocks away, Janice heard the blast, and not long after, the sirens.

Marie was safe, Janice was safe, the rest of Nancy's family was now safe, and Rocky was no longer a threat. Rocky the Dog had outsmarted himself.

Win-win.

***

Special Bonus Story

Although this extra story concerns a crime, it's a different type of crime story, with other elements. Something a little out of the ordinary, with a twist. Hope you like it.

The Maids

Old Harlow Coffey was in charge of the docks while the other men and boats were out fishing. After they'd caught their limit for the day, they'd all head over to the mainland to unload and sell their catch. Then they'd stream back, sometimes in a convoy, to return to Outer Rock Haven close to suppertime to gather at the one island bar and drink away some of their pay before going home to their families.

So until they returned, Harlow didn't have much to do. It was just after noon, and he was surprised to hear the chug of an engine and see a strange boat come into view and approach the dock. The island didn't get visitors, and few islanders left, except for weekly postal and grocery runs, or an occasional doctor visit.

Harlow put down his mug of coffee laced with bourbon, stretched, and limped his way out on the dock. The craft wasn't a fishing vessel, just a small dive boat. The lone man behind the wheel cut the engine and the vessel drifted sideways to gently tap the dock's rubber tire bumpers. It was a nice soft landing, so Harlow knew the man had experience.

The man tossed Harlow a line, and Harlow secured the bow of the craft to the dock piling. The man jumped onto the dock with a line in his hand and secured the stern to another piling. He was tall, sturdy-looking, and moved well.

"Hey there," said Harlow. "Can I help you?"

"All set," said the man. He made to walk on past.

"You got some business here?"

The man turned back to look Harlow up and down. "Nothing to concern you." He walked down the dock.

Harlow took off his long-billed cap and scratched his head. He thought maybe he'd better go get someone to deal with this.

The man walked up the street away from the waterfront and went into the Dockside, the island's only bar and eatery.

Inside was dark and quiet. Three older men were drinking, two hunched over at the bar and one by himself over near the pool table. Betty, the fifty-something woman who ran the place, had a bar towel over her shoulder. When the stranger sat down at the bar, she did a doubletake, arching her eyebrows as her mouth made a little O.

"Uh, hello. Can I help you?"

"Can I get a draft and a cheeseburger?"

"Sure." She poured the draft and set it before him. "How you want that done?"

"Medium's fine."

Betty went to cook the burger. With almost never a lunch to serve, she was the only one on until five, when Faye would join her for the rush as the men returned. She slapped a patty on the grill, put two bun halves on the warm side to toast, and added some potato chips and a pickle to a plate.

The stranger said nothing, and neither did anyone else in the place, but all eyes were on him. He drank his beer and looked around, but no one met his gaze. Betty flipped the burger, added a slice of orange-colored cheese, and stepped back to talk.

"What brings you out this way?"

"Lunch. I was out on the water and got hungry."

"Oh. You're not a fisherman?"

"Nope. Run a dive business down in Gloucester."

"Mass, huh?"

"Yup." He offered nothing else. He was as tight-lipped as any islander.

"Out checking the coast?"

The man smiled. "Think my burger might be ready. Don't want it too overdone."

Betty looked back at the grill, nodded, and went to assemble the meal. She placed the plate before the man, and a paper napkin beside it.

"We don't get a lot of visitors. Why'd you wind up here?"

The man smiled again. "Got any ketchup?"

Betty brought back a bottle and set it down. The man nodded and shook some onto his burger, seeming to have forgot her previous question. His gaze was sharp, though, taking everything in, so he hadn't forgot, he just didn't want to talk. He took a bite, and Betty knew there was no more chance for questions until he was done.

The man by the pool table held up his glass, and Betty went to give him a refill.

"Who is he? What's he want?" The man almost hissed his words.

"No idea. Ain't much of a talker." Betty went back behind the bar, and saw the stranger was almost done. She indicated his empty glass. "Another?"

He nodded. She set a fresh one before him and removed the empty. He pushed his plate away and she went to take it. She was burning with curiosity, but sensed the man would only give real answers when he wanted. He took a deep swallow from his glass and turned on his stool to address the room.

"Which one of you's Cutty Jackson?"

Three gazes shot to one of the men at the bar before quickly looking away. The one they'd looked at shrank into himself, as if trying to turn invisible.

The stranger got off his stool and put his arm around Cutty. "Let's you and me have a little parley. Miss, could we get this man a double whiskey, please? He looks a little pale."

The stranger almost lifted Cutty off the stool and semi-dragged him over to a booth in the corner. Betty pursed her lips but said nothing. She shrugged, poured the whiskey, and took it over. The stranger smiled up at her. "Just a friendly little chat, that's all."

When she had walked away, Cutty pulled the glass to his mouth, none too steady.

"What you want? I ain't done nothin."

The stranger leaned in close. I want to know where you were last Saturday, Cutty."

Cutty's eyes widened, showing white. He licked his lips. "I uh, I was sick."

"Sick, huh? What kind of sick?"

"Just didn't feel well, that's all."

"Too sick to work, huh?"

"That's right."

"You been back to work since?"

"No. I'm retired."

"Kind of sudden, wasn't it?"

Cutty shrugged and drained the last of his whiskey.

The stranger held up his arm and called over to the bar. "Miss, how about another double for my friend here."

Betty threw down her bar towel and quickly walked over. "He's had enough, mister. He should go home now. Isn't that right, Cutty?"

Cutty had his head down, mumbling something.

The stranger was still smiling, but his eyes were hard. "Why, it's almost as if you don't want me talking to poor Cutty here. Almost as if you thought he had some dark secret to tell me. That about it? Some dirty island secret you don't want scared little Cutty to spill when he's had a few too many?"

"Time for you to leave too, mister. Here's your check."

The stranger got to his feet suddenly, looming over her. Betty swallowed, but crossed her arms and stood her ground. "Door's that way."

The man threw a twenty-dollar bill on the table. "Keep the change. I know you people like your blood money." He left without a backward glance. The other men in the place rushed over to quiz Cutty on what the stranger had said.

Outside, the stranger started walking inland, with a number of people watching. Some followed his progress to a side lane off the main street, to a small cottage at the end of the lane. They saw him open the door and go in.

After a hurried consultation, one man approached the cottage and knocked, as a small knot of women watched from a few yards away, close enough to hear.

The door swung open, and the stranger filled the doorway. His gaze was not friendly, but the man at the door plastered on a smile and stuck out his hand. "Hello there. I'm Wally Eastman,

I kind of oversee things here on the island. Can I ask what you're doing here?"

"I think you just did." The man did not offer to shake. Eastman lowered his hand.

"How did you get in? This isn't your house."

The man looked around. "Whose house is it?"

Eastman blinked. "Danny Sorrell's."

"Oh? And where is he?"

Eastman tried for a somber expression. "I'm afraid he drowned. Last Saturday."

"Drowned, huh? That's a real shame. Guess he won't be needing this place, then."

Eastman opened his mouth to protest, but the stranger cut him off. "I'm his cousin Parker. Lawyer gave me the key. Where is he buried, then? I want to go visit."

"Uh, we never recovered his body."

The stranger adopted a look of mock surprise. "You didn't? But you just told me he drowned. How do you know that if you never found him?"

"We found his boat, three miles out, adrift."

"Huh. How long did the Coast Guard run their search?"

"We didn't call them. But we had all the boats on the island searching. We keep to ourselves here."

"How do you know he wasn't out there, with a life preserver or something, hanging onto a cooler?"

"We know these waters, and the currents. We'd have found him if he hadn't gone under."

"You seem mighty sure of that. What was he doing out there, all by himself?"

"Fishing, like he always did."

"Really? All by himself? Kind of unusual, isn't it?"

"His mate got sick."

"Ah, yes, the mysterious Mr. Cutty, who no one wants me to talk to. How unlucky Danny goes overboard the one day Mr. Cutty is not with him."

"It happens, unfortunately. The sea takes its toll."

"Danny's been on the water since he was born. And you're telling me he was alone and careless enough to go over. Seems kind of fishy there, Eastman."

"We all mourn him. He was one of us. We put up a memorial to him over at the church."

"I'd like to see that."

"I'll walk you over."

The inside of Our Ladies of the Sea had five pews per side and a table set off on the right with a picture of Danny, some flowers, candles, and a few offerings of trinkets and memorials. Parker took it in. He looked at the stained-glass window and saw three women depicted from the waist up, in water, with long flowing hair covering their unclad torsos.

"What is this, a coffeehouse or a church?"

"The Three Sisters founded this island. And as you see, we remember Danny and grieve for him."

Parker nodded. "And all went about your business rather quickly." He turned suddenly. "I want to see his boat. That was it to the side of the dock, wasn't it?"

"Uh, I'm not sure that's a good idea."

"How come? You hiding something?"

"Of course not." Eastman sighed. "We just don't want to upset people."

"Bet the Coast Guard would like to have a look at it, missing fisherman and all. Shall I call them?"

Eastman chewed his lip. "I guess you won't be happy until you see it for yourself. Fine."

They walked back down to dockside. Harlow met them.

Eastman spoke. "We're going to see Danny's boat, Harlow. This is his cousin from down in Massachusetts."

They walked over, and Parker stepped on board while the two men watched from the dock, and more women watched from the shore. Parker closely examined everything: the rail, the scuppers, the deck, the nets, the enclosed wheelhouse. He opened the fuel tanks, peered in, and read the gauges.

"Satisfied?" Eastman looked hopeful.

"You say it was found three miles out?"

"That's right."

"That burns fuel. These tanks are full."

"Well, ah, maybe someone filled it up when they got it back here."

"Uh huh. What happened to his catch?"

"What?"

"You said he was out fishing. So he should have put his nets out, yet here they are, all nice and clean, like they never went in that day. Or maybe some kind soul took care of them, too, as well as filling his tanks with fuel. So what happened to his catch?"

"I don't know," Eastman shrugged. "Maybe he didn't get a chance to get them out."

"Sure," said Parker. "Heads three miles out, by himself, stops, and whoops, over he goes. He was a strong swimmer, but no, by golly, down he goes like a stone. Some of you come along and shrug, and make a half-assed pretense of a search, and declare him gone."

"I don't like your tone, mister, or what you're getting at."

"Ain't that just a shame."

"He was one of us, and you're a stranger. Maybe you better go now."

Parker sprang onto the dock and stared down Eastman until the smaller man looked away. Parker shook his head and walked back along the dock to his boat, undid the stern line, threw it onto his boat, undid the bow line, and jumped aboard. He started the engine and eased away from the dock, not looking back.

"Think he'll cause more trouble?" Harlow looked at Eastman.

"I'm afraid we may not have seen the last of Mr. Nosy Parker."

Of course there was a meeting on the island that night when the men returned. Things were rather subdued for a Saturday evening, and they drew straws to see who would patrol the offshore waters the next day in case Parker came back. They got out their rifles and pistols and cleaned them, loading up in case there was a need.

Sunday morning found most of the town in church, making more prayers than usual. At the end of the long service, a man slammed through the doors.

"He's out there," he yelled out to the congregation. "Sonofabitch is out there with dive equipment."

"Let's go," the fishermen rose and hurried out.

Harlow turned to Eastman. "Won't the Ladies take care of him?"

"What if they get angry that strangers came? Our bargain is to keep people away. We can't take that chance."

Out on the water, Parker and his friend prepared for their dive, with two other men to keep watch up top. Both of them had pistols in holsters by their side.

"What do we need spearguns for," asked Parker's friend. "There's no sharks up this way."

"You wouldn't believe me if I told you."

"You're not talking about that stupid story Danny told that night when he was drunk, are you? Come on, you know he was just pulling your leg."

"Maybe, but those people are hiding something, and we need to see what it is. Maybe there's a wreck to salvage, or something like that. I don't want to take any chances, so keep your eyes open down there."

Minutes later, they were about forty feet down, their headlamps providing a tunnel of light through the gloom. They dropped underwater flares for a wider range of illumination.

Parker was on the alert, and so saw the thing rushing towards him, taloned arms outstretched to strike and a mouthful of sharp teeth in a white face. He aimed and fired the speargun, and the thing stopped as a trail of blood became highlighted in the beam of light. Parker turned to his friend, who was obscured by something else attacking him. Parker drew his knife and stabbed through a mass of hair, sinking the knife deep into a back. The thing twisted away and swam off. Parker saw his friend was hurt, and they began their ascent to the surface.

When they broke the surface, Parker saw one of the men pointing a pistol at him. "Don't shoot! It's me."

"Jesus, Parker, what was that thing? It got Harry with a trident for God's sake. He's hurt, but he'll live. I put a coupla rounds into it, and it screamed and swam off."

"You call for the cavalry?"

"You bet. And radar shows nine boats from the island headed our way."

"I figured. Let's patch these guys up until the help arrives."

They helped the two injured men, and got the bleeding stopped, keeping an eye out for any more attacks. Parker looked up and saw the first of the fishing boats racing towards them. More were behind it. He picked up the mike for the radio when there was a squawk.

"Let me guess," he depressed the call button and spoke into the mike. "The Outer Rock Haven Avoidance Committee."

"You are trespassing. Put up your hands and prepare to be boarded."

"Trespassing? Don't think so. This was Danny's area. He showed me on a map."

"That area has been reapportioned, and you are not authorized to be in the area."

"You mean because of your little secret? Well, secret's out boys. They attacked us. At least one of them's dead, and the others wounded."

There was a shriek on the other end. "What have you done? You stupid man, what have you done?"

"You shouldn't have killed Danny."

"He lost the lottery. He knew what that meant. He sacrificed himself to save us all."

"You picked the wrong person to sacrifice."

"Everyone else had wives and kids. He had no family left on the island."

"Ah, so you rigged the lottery. Wasn't random at all, was it?"

There was a silence. "You're going to be real sorry you came."

"Don't think so. See that plane overhead? That's the spotter. Coast Guard cutters are on their way. I thought you people might try something, so we had them waiting and ready. You can try to fight them if you want, but it won't go well for you. Might want to tuck your tail between your legs and go home and say goodbye to your loved ones, because you're all going to prison."

There was nothing else on the radio. Parker looked out, and the boats had stopped racing closer. They cut their engines, waiting.

Some time later, Parker sat at a table in a small room on the mainland. He'd been waiting in this room for well over an hour. The door finally opened and a man in a suit came in, holding a folder. He sat across from Parker and put the folder down. He took out a document and pushed it over to Parker, adding a pen.

"Who the hell are you, and why have I been waiting? How are my friends? We're not the criminals here."

"Mr. Parker, you've caused a lot of problems. They're fine. You need to read that over and sign it."

"Why? What is it? A statement?"

"Sort of. It's a confession and an agreement."

"Confession of what? I didn't do anything."

"But you did. You brought to life something that wasn't supposed to be."

"You mean those things that attacked us?"

"The Navy needs to study these creatures, and we need to keep it secret. That's where you and your friends come in."

"What do you mean?"

"You're going to want to tell everyone what you found. This agreement says you won't."

"Why not?"

"National Security. This says you acknowledge you were sabotaging a government experiment, and you will not be prosecuted as long as this never becomes public knowledge."

"You can't be serious. That was no experiment."

"Your say-so against the Navy's. Pretty serious charge."

"I have my rights."

"Is that so? We have black sites around the globe, Mr. Parker. Mention even a whisper of this and you and your friends will disappear one night and never be seen again. While word gets out about your mental instability. Your friends have families, don't they? Wives, kids, parents still living. Would be terrible to rip them from the ones they love. And they've all signed this, so you're the only one left."

Parker ran his hands through his hair. "What about the islanders? They all know. It's their cult that got Danny killed."

"They've had a long-standing agreement. It's how they stay alive, fishing from that little rock. The men will be punished for the death of your cousin. As you suspected, they rigged the lottery so he would be the one sacrificed. With the men gone, the source of their livelihood, the ones left will have nothing. They certainly can't grow enough food to survive. We'll probably relocate them. But none of them will ever breathe a word, trust me."

"Why are you doing this?"

"These creatures are pretty extraordinary. They could help us out in our war."

"The war that never ends and never runs out of enemies?"

"Just so. That about sums it up, Mr. Parker. So, do you choose freedom to live your life, or a futile gesture that makes you and your friends go away from public view. Forever."

Parker picked up the pen, glaring at the man. "Like your work, you bastard?"

"I've been called much worse, I assure you. And I've certainly done much worse."

With no good choice left, Parker signed. The Maids of the Sea would remain a secret from the outside world.

***

AFTERWORD

Like many mystery writers, I started early in the genre, reading the Hardy Boys, Nancy Drew, and Encyclopedia Brown. I went on to Sherlock Holmes and Agatha Christie, of course, and discovered the darker side of crime and mystery: Dashiell Hammett, Raymond Chandler, Jim Thompson, Mickey Spillane, John D. MacDonald, Robert B. Parker, Elmore Leonard, Robert Crais, James Lee Burke. There are so many more, but you have dozens of works there to choose from, so much of the best. Masters of their craft, at creating a story that interests the reader and doesn't disappoint.

In no way do I invite comparisons, though I do hope these tales pique your interest and make you want more. In that vein, I have other works of crime and mystery, and I invite you to sample some. Following is the first chapter of the first book of the Zack Taylor series, a protagonist inspired by and in homage to John D. MacDonald's Travis McGee.

If you like the writing and would like to tackle something longer, there's the Zack

Taylor mystery series, available in print, ebook, and audiobook.

Troubled ex-con Zack Taylor is haunted by the accidental death of his brother years before. Zack's guilt and anger have pushed him into a shadowy, wandering life, with little purpose and few attachments. When he hears of the death of his close friend Ben Sterling, a supposed gunshot suicide, Zack finds he now has a purpose— to find out what happened.

Then his purpose becomes an obsession.

Here's a sample:

A Memory of Grief

Pain can be nature's way of telling you that you have done something really stupid. So I was getting quite a lecture. There was no way I could have won the fight, and sure, I'd known that going in. But I gave it my best. Then came the kick to my head, so fast that I had no time to block or duck. For the next hour, I'd simply tried to reassemble my thoughts.

Now I sat on a barstool, aching down to the bone with bruises and stiff limbs, holding an ice-filled bar towel against the cut over my eye.

The coolness felt good. My head throbbed, but by some miracle I didn't seem to have a concussion, so I counted my blessings.

We were at a private nightclub near the edge of Miami's Little Havana. At Hernando's Hideaway, I was in charge of security, taking care of whatever trouble came up. Here in Miami, there was always trouble.

The mirror behind the bar showed the reflection of people around me. Hernando had permitted my rooting section to come in with me, even though the place didn't open for another few hours. The pain took all my focus for the moment, so I didn't want to talk to anyone. But I couldn't ignore Esteban, watching me from behind the bar.

"Your face looks hurted, Zack. Are you okay?"

I wasn't, but I didn't want to worry the kid.

"I'm fine."

"Want more ice?"

The water dripping down between my fingers had gone tepid.

"Sure."

He took the wrap from me, shook out a few slivers of ice, wrung the cloth out, and meticulously refilled it with cubes from behind the bar.

"Thanks," I said when he handed it back. I put it to my bruised flesh and sat very still. Snippets of conversation began to register.

"When Zack landed that kick in the second round, I thought he had him."

"Nah, man," said someone. "That just woke Gutierrez up, and he poured it on. Man, that guy's gonna be world champ someday."

"You did us all proud today, Zack," someone else said, slapping my back, which jolted me with fresh pain. "How about a drink?"

Esteban frowned and shook his head. "No, no, no. Zack don't drink. Zack never drinks."

The guy looked at Esteban and then at me. "Special Ed here for real? You work in a *bar.*"

I shrugged, sending another wave of hurt cascading through my injured cranium. I moaned softly, and my mind drifted away again. No one bothered me for a few minutes, and my head finally stopped hammering so hard.

Esteban placed an envelope on the bar in front of me.

"Zack, look. A letter came for you."

I looked at it, puzzled. Only my friend Ben knew where I was, and he always phoned, never wrote. He was supposed to call later to find out how I'd done. We'd have a good laugh when I explained how badly I'd got my butt whipped.

I put down the cloth and picked up the envelope. There was my name, in spiky handwriting, with no return address and a postmark from North Carolina.

Since my arms felt tired and heavy from the pounding I'd taken, it took a fumbling minute to pull out a newspaper clipping and a folded sheet of paper. The clipping fell, and fluttered to the floor. Somebody reached down to pick it up while I tried to read what looked like a letter. Moisture from the bar had mottled the paper with large, wet blots.

"You dropped this," someone said. I waved him off, trying to concentrate on making sense of the letter. He spoke again. "Don't you know a guy named Benjamin Sterling?"

"Yeah, Ben's my best friend," I said. I put down the letter and turned in the direction of the voice, my head pounding in protest. "Is he on the phone?"

There was no answer, just a sudden, strange silence. The guy looked away, and thrust the clipping at someone else. That guy frowned while reading it, then looked up at me.

"What is it?" I asked.

Neither of them spoke. The second guy put the piece of paper on the bar, and they both silently slipped back into the crowd. Wondering at their strange behavior, I picked up the clipping. It was from the Press-Herald in Portland, Maine. It said that Benjamin Sterling, a cook at the Pine Haven resort, had died from a self-inflicted gunshot wound, after a brief period in the Portland hospital for food poisoning.

No. It wasn't true, couldn't be true. No way. It was some other Ben Sterling. "No, no," I rasped. It was a joke, a sick joke.

Someone put a hand on my shoulder. I shrugged it away, angry. I grabbed the letter from the bar. My hands were shaking as I read it:

Dear Zak,

We never got along but Ben always sed that we were the only two who mattered in his life. I rote to say how sorry I am about his dying. I still cant believe he done it. Shows you just never know. Thay called me from Main and buryed him in the city cimatarry. I woulda called you but dint have no number, just this address.

Maureen

P.S. I did love him, but we was just too differnt.

I felt cold inside, confused. I didn't believe it. What the hell was Ben's ex-wife up to? I read it again, and found myself trembling. My jaw was clenched so tight my teeth hurt. Killed himself? No damn way. I scanned the clipping again, trying to make sense of it, for Ben would never do that. Not ever.

I tried to stand, but dizziness forced me back onto the stool. People mumbled condolences, but their words slid off me like cold raindrops. I tuned them out. I needed a drink to push this away. My past came rushing back once more, after all the years of trying to forget. The floodwaters of memory swept in; I went under.

Some time later, the crowd was gone. Without people here, the room was too empty and still. It reminded me of the hollow ache inside.

Esteban stood staring at me, not moving. The pounding in my head had subsided to a dull ache, and the dizziness was gone. I wondered how long he and I had been like this.

I started breathing again. "Is Hernando upstairs?"

Esteban nodded, then shifted his eyes downward. "The bad man's with him."

"Raul?" I growled. "Did he push you again?"

"No. He only called me a stupid retard. It's okay."

"It's not okay!" I roared, slamming my hands to the bar and jumping up. The stool crashed to the floor, and Esteban backed away, looking terrified. I closed my eyes and ground my hands into my face. I couldn't stop shaking. I forced calm into my voice.

"I'm sorry, Esteban. I didn't mean to yell. Forget what he said. There's nothing wrong with you." I looked toward the back, to the stairs leading to Hernando's office. "He's just a bad man who enjoys hurting other people. And he has to stop."

I felt the old rage stir within me, a beast now unchained and hungry. Something was going to happen. Something bad.

***

ABOUT THE AUTHOR

Dale T. Phillips has published novels, story collections, non-fiction, and over 80 short stories. Stephen King was Dale's college writing teacher, and since that time, Dale has found time to appear on stage, television, in an independent feature film, and compete on *Jeopardy* (losing in a spectacular fashion). He co-wrote and acted in a short political satire film. He's traveled to all 50 states, Mexico, Canada, and through Europe.

Connect Online:
Website: http://www.daletphillips.com
Blog: http://daletphillips@blogspot.com
Twitter: DalePhillips2

Try these other works by Dale T. Phillips

Shadow of the Wendigo (Supernatural Thriller)
Neptune City (Mystery)
Locust Time (Suspense)
Desert Heat (Mystery- coming Spring 2023)

The Zack Taylor Mystery Series
A Darkened Room
A Sharp Medicine
A Certain Slant of Light
A Shadow on the Wall
A Fall From Grace
A Memory of Grief

Story Collections
The Big Book of Genre Stories (Different Genres)
Halls of Horror (Horror)
Deadly Encounters (3 Zack Taylor Mystery/Crime Tales)
The Return of Fear (Scary Stories)
Five Fingers of Fear (Scary Stories)
Jumble Sale (Different Genres)
Crooked Paths (Mystery/Crime)
More Crooked Paths (Mystery/Crime)
The Last Crooked Paths (Mystery/Crime)
Fables and Fantasies (Fantasy)
More Fables and Fantasies (Fantasy)
The Last Fables and Fantasies (Fantasy)
Strange Tales (Magic Realism, Paranormal)
Apocalypse Tango (End of the World)

Non-fiction Career Help
How to be a Successful Indie Writer
How to Improve Your Interviewing Skills

With Other Authors

Rogue Wave: Best New England Crime Stories 2015
Red Dawn: Best New England Crime Stories 2016
Windward: Best New England Crime Stories 2017

Sign up for my newsletter to get special offers
http://www.daletphillips.com

Made in the USA
Middletown, DE
29 October 2023

41432516R00096